A GIFT OF DEATH

In Part 1, John Saul introduced us to the village of Blackstone, where a shadowed, evil hand in the old Asylum began to dispense mysterious gifts to various unsuspecting residents . . . with grim consequences. First came the doll, which tore apart the lives of the local contractor, Bill McGuire, his pregnant wife, and their child.

In Part 2, the president of the First National Bank of Blackstone, Jules Hartwick, discovered a pink beribboned package in his wife's car. The silver locket inside unleashed a murderous, maniacal rage.

In Part 3, at a flea market, library assistant Rebecca Morrison found an antique cigarette lighter in the shape of a dragon that breathed fire. She gave it to her wayward cousin and ignited a fiery and very deadly reunion.

Now the dark figure deep inside the Asylum selects an elegant monogrammed handkerchief. Pity the poor soul who receives it. . . .

THE BLACKSTONE CHRONICLES
IN THE SHADOW OF EVIL:
THE HANDKERCHIEF

By John Saul:

*Published by Fawcett Books

THE BLACKSTONE CHRONICLES

PART 4
IN THE SHADOW OF EVIL: THE HANDKERCHIEF

John Saul

FAWCETT CREST • NEW YORK

A Fawcett Crest Book
Published by Ballantine Books
Copyright © 1997 by John Saul

Map by Christine Levis

http://www.randomhouse.com

Library of Congress Catalog Card Number: 97-90038

ISBN 0-449-22788-X

Manufactured in the United States of America

First Edition: May 1997

10 9 8 7 6 5 4 3 2 1

For Linda with
hearts and flowers

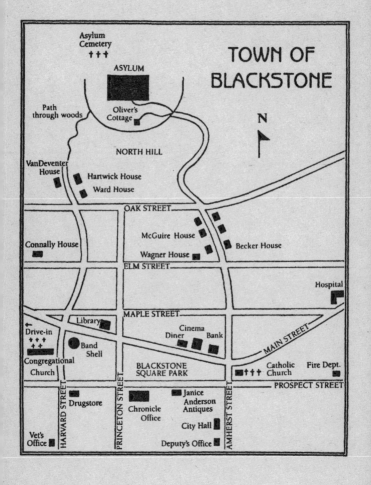

TOWN OF BLACKSTONE

Asylum
Cemetery
✝ ✝ ✝

ASYLUM

Path
through woods

Oliver's
Cottage

N

NORTH HILL

VanDeventer
House

Hartwick House

Ward House

OAK STREET

McGuire House

Becker House

Connally House

Wagner House

ELM STREET

Hospital

MAPLE STREET

Library

Cinema

Drive-in
✝ ✝ ✝
✝ ✝

Diner

Bank

MAIN STREET

Band
Shell

Congregational
Church

BLACKSTONE
SQUARE PARK

Catholic
✝ ✝ ✝ Church

Fire Dept.

PROSPECT STREET

Drugstore

Chronicle
Office

Janice
Anderson
Antiques

City Hall

Vet's
Office

Deputy's Office

HARVARD STREET

PRINCETON STREET

AMHERST STREET

The Connally Family

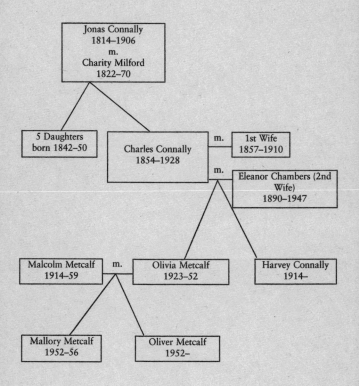

Jonas Connally
1814–1906
m.
Charity Milford
1822–70

5 Daughters
born 1842–50

Charles Connally
1854–1928

m. 1st Wife
1857–1910

m. Eleanor Chambers (2nd Wife)
1890–1947

Malcolm Metcalf
1914–59

m. Olivia Metcalf
1923–52

Harvey Connally
1914–

Mallory Metcalf
1952–56

Oliver Metcalf
1952–

Prelude

Once again the time had come.

The moon, high in the early spring sky, silvered the long-concealed room with a glow that lent the objects within the quality of a bas relief. The dark figure, though, saw nothing this night save the handkerchief. Its soft folds hung gracefully from his surgically gloved fingers, its pale linen seeming to shine with a luminescence of its own. Nor was he aware that beyond the stone walls the winter's stillness was occasionally pierced by the first tentative mating calls of insects and frogs slowly emerging from their seasonal torpor; within the building's dark confines the silence of nearly half a century still reigned.

Enclosed in that silvery silence, the dark figure stroked the linen lovingly, and from the depths of his mind, a memory began to emerge. . . .

Prologue

*T*he woman rose languorously from her bed, letting her fingers trail over the smoothness of the silk sheets and caress the softness of the cashmere blankets before she drifted across the room to gaze out the window. It was late in the afternoon. Below, two of her gardeners tended to the rosebushes she'd laid out last year, while another trimmed the low box hedge. Some of her guests were playing badminton on the broad lawn beyond the rose garden, and when one of them looked up, she waved gaily. For a moment she toyed with the idea of dressing and going out to join them, but then she changed her mind.

Better to stay in her boudoir, resting and enjoying her privacy before tonight's festivities began.

What was it to be tonight?

A formal dinner, with dancing afterward?

Or a fancy-dress ball, with supper at midnight and a champagne breakfast served just after dawn?

She couldn't remember just now, but it didn't matter really, for one of her maids would remind her when it was time for her to dress for the evening.

Turning away from the window, she wafted back to the bed and stretched out once more, picking up the square of finest linen she'd been embroidering for several weeks now.

It was edged with lace, every stitch perfectly worked into a floral design so exquisitely wrought that she could *almost smell the flowers' scent. In one corner she was working a single initial, an ornate R to signify the rank of the handkerchief's eventual recipient. Regina.*

The queen would be pleased with her gift, and perhaps even summon her to court—a most pleasurable diversion, inasmuch as it had been months since she'd been away from her own country seat.

Spreading the handkerchief on her lap, she set about the final embroidery. Surrounding the R was another intricate pattern of flowers, these woven into the linen in the finest and palest of silk thread, lending the handkerchief a faint aura of color that was almost more illusion than reality. The stitching was so delicate that it seemed to emerge from the weave itself, and each side was as perfect as the other. Even the monogram had been mirrored so the handkerchief had no wrong side.

An hour later, as she worked the last thread into the design, then snipped its end away so deftly that it instantly disappeared into the pattern, she heard a sharp rap at the door, announcing the arrival of her maid. Setting the handkerchief aside, she drew her robe more tightly around her throat. "You may come in," she announced.

The door opened and the servant appeared, bearing a silver tray upon which she could see a plate covered by an ornately engraved silver dome.

An afternoon repast.

Which meant that tonight would be the fancy-dress ball. She must begin thinking about a costume.

"What have you brought me, Marie?" the woman asked. "A pâté perhaps? Some caviar?"

The nurse's hands tightened on the metal tray.

Pâté?

Caviar?

Not likely.

And not that it mattered either. Even if she'd brought half a pound of pâté de foie gras or a whole can of Beluga caviar, it wouldn't be good enough for this one! She hadn't eaten anything at all for a week. And how many times had she told the woman her name was Clara, not Marie? "It's spaghetti," she said as she bent at the waist, intending to set the tray down on the woman's lap. "With some nice salad with oranges, and a roll."

"Be careful!" the woman ordered, her voice sharp. "This robe was handmade for me, and if you stain it—"

"I know." The nurse sighed, straightening again, the tray still in her hands. "I'll be dismissed." She eyed the rough terry-cloth robe the patient wore over her flannel nightgown, and wondered just what material the woman's delusions had created. Silk? Ermine? Who knew? Or cared? "And if you spill it all over yourself, don't try to blame me. It won't be anybody's fault but your own."

The patient drew herself up, her eyes narrowing into slits of anger. "I will not be spoken to like—"

"You'll be spoken to any way I want," the nurse interrupted. "And if you're smart, you'll eat this."

Finally setting the metal tray on the patient's lap, she lifted the cover off the plate.

The silver dome lifted to reveal a tangle of worms writhing in a pool of blood, and a rat, its red eyes glaring balefully up at her. As she hurled the silver tray off her lap and flung it aside, the rat leaped away to scuttle across the floor, and the blood and worms cascaded down Marie's uniform. Feeling no sympathy at all for the servant who had subjected her to such torture, the woman reached out to slap the hapless girl, but to her utter astonishment, the maid caught her wrist, immobi-

lizing it in a grip so strong the woman was suddenly terrified her bones might break.

"How dare—" she began, but the maid cut in without
letting her finish.

"Don't 'how dare' me, Miss High-and-Mighty! I've
had just about enough of your acting like I'm your servant. Look what you've done to my uniform! How would
you like it if these were your clothes?"

Rendered speechless by the impertinence, the woman
watched as the maid dropped her wrist, then reached out
and snatched up the handkerchief she'd finished embroidering only a few minutes ago. As the woman looked on
in horror from her bed, the servant pressed the fine linen
square to her chest, using it to soak up the blood on her
uniform.

"Stop that!" she demanded. "Stop that this instant!
You'll ruin it!"

The nurse glowered furiously at the patient as she wiped
away the mess of spaghetti and tomato sauce that was
still dripping down her brand new uniform. She'd bought
it only last week and was wearing it for the first time that
day. "You think you can get away with anything, don't
you?" she asked. "Well, you're about to find out who
runs this place, and it isn't you." Leaving the patient
cowering in her bed, the nurse strode out of the room,
returning a few moments later with an orderly and a
doctor. While the orderly mopped the splatter of spaghetti off the linoleum floor, the nurse recounted the inci-
dent to the doctor. "I suppose if she won't eat, it's really
none of my business," she finished. "But I don't have to
stand for her throwing her food at me."

The doctor, whose eyes had been fixed on the patient
throughout the nurse's recitation, smiled thinly. "No,"

*he agreed, "you certainly don't. And it's certainly time
she began eating too, don't you think?"*

*For a moment the nurse said nothing, but then, as she
realized what the doctor was saying, she smiled for the
first time since entering the room a few minutes earlier.
"Yes," she said, "I certainly do!"*

*With the aid of two more orderlies, the doctor and the
nurse secured the struggling patient to her bed with thick
nylon straps. When the woman was totally immobilized,
the doctor instructed the aides to hold the patient's
mouth open.*

*As the woman moaned and struggled, then began to
gag, the doctor inserted a thick plastic feeding tube
through her mouth, down her throat, and into her
stomach.*

"There," he said. "That should do it."

*Before he left the nurse to begin feeding the immobi-
lized patient, he stooped down and picked up the soiled
handkerchief from the floor. Holding it gingerly between
his thumb and forefinger, he gazed at the elaborately
embroidered initial and the perfectly worked lace.
"Interesting," he said, more to himself than to the nurse.
"I wonder who she thought she was making it for."
Crushing the handkerchief into a shapeless mass, he
stuffed it into the pocket of his white coat and left
the room.*

*The woman in the bed tried to cry out, tried to beg
him not to take away the beautiful handkerchief she'd
spent so many weeks making, but the tube in her throat
turned her plea into nothing more than an incomprehensible moan.*

She never saw the handkerchief again.

*A month later, when she was finally released from
the bonds that held her to the bed, she waited until she
was alone, then used the belt of her terry-cloth robe to
hang herself from the clothes hook on the back of her
door.*

* * *

Still gazing at the handkerchief, the dark figure let his finger trace the perfectly embroidered R that had been worked into one of its corners.

The letter itself told him who its recipient must be.

All he regretted was that he couldn't deliver it personally. Still, he knew how to guide the handkerchief to its destination, and who its bearer would be. . . .

Chapter 1

*O*liver Metcalf had spring fever. There simply wasn't any other way to describe it. The first symptoms had appeared early that morning, when he found himself lingering in his kitchen over an extra cup of coffee while he watched a pair of robins begin their courtship. It was the first morning that was warm enough to open the window, and the air was redolent with the musky smell of leaves that had been slowly decomposing under the winter's finally vanished blanket of snow. Inhaling the scent of spring, he felt the first faint urge to take the day off. He ignored the urge, of course, since today was Tuesday, the deadline for putting this week's edition of the *Chronicle* to bed, but the seductive sense of lassitude that had come over him as the birds' songs drifted into his kitchen only increased a few minutes later as he set out down Harvard Street toward the village at the foot of North Hill. His pace, which he'd fully intended to keep aerobically brisk, had slowed to a leisurely stroll, and he kept pausing to admire the crocuses that were blooming everywhere, and the daffodil shoots that seemed to have shot up at least six inches just since yesterday.

By the time he came to Main Street, a stop at the Red Hen had seemed utterly imperative, and this morning's fifteen minutes of gossip disguised as "networking" had somehow managed to stretch out to half an hour. Even then, Bill McGuire and Ed Becker were still at the counter when he left, postponing the start of their workday under the guise of a serious conversation regarding the financing for Blackstone Center and when it might finally come through. That Melissa Holloway, who had officially been appointed permanent president of the bank at the last meeting of its board of directors, had told them they could count on no approvals any earlier than June seemed to cut no ice with Bill and Ed. But then, it was that kind of morning: today everyone seemed to prefer speculation over actual labor. When Oliver finally arrived at the *Chronicle*, it was more of the same.

"Everyone wants to know when you're going to run a story about what's been going on," Lois Martin said as he opened the office door. "I just got another call—this time from Edna Burnham. She says everyone in town is talking, and it's up to you to stop it."

The temperature of Oliver's pleasant springtime mood notched down to a wintry chill. He knew perfectly well what Lois was talking about: a day hadn't gone by in the month since Martha Ward had burned her own house to the ground and perished in the flames that someone hadn't called the paper demanding to know what—exactly—the connection was between the suicides of Elizabeth McGuire, Jules Hartwick, and Martha Ward. As far as Oliver could see, there was no connection at all.

A few odd coincidences, perhaps, but nothing more than that.

It was Edna's contention, Oliver knew, that there was ominous significance in the fact that all three of the suicides had occurred shortly after a full moon. But the term *lunacy* had been around in one form or another for millennia, and given that all three of Blackstone's tragic victims had been under one form of stress or another, Oliver wasn't willing to call the full moon a causative factor for any of them. A trigger, possibly, but certainly no more.

Still, if Edna Burnham was demanding answers, it meant the talk was starting to get even more serious than Oliver had thought.

"Does she have a new theory, or is she just upset?" he asked.

Lois Martin hesitated before answering his question, and when she did, her eyes didn't quite meet Oliver's. "She's wondering if it might not all go back to the Asylum somehow."

"The Asylum," Oliver repeated. "And did she say what put that idea in her mind?"

Lois's eyes finally met his. "A few things, actually," she said, picking up a pad on which she'd scribbled some notes when old Mrs. Burnham had called. The phone had been ringing off the hook when Lois arrived that morning. "First off," Lois told him, "there's the anonymous gifts. Edna claims to have heard whisperings about weird things that turned up, first at the McGuires', then at Jules's house and at Martha's. She says no one knows where they came from."

A look of disbelief came over Oliver's face. "Come on! What kind of things?"

"Well, Bill McGuire was talking about a doll that showed up in the mail a few days before Elizabeth killed herself, and Rebecca told her about a gold cigarette lighter—"

"I know where that came from," Oliver told her. "No mystery there. Rebecca and I found it at the flea market."

"I know, I know." She held up a hand to stop his protests. "Edna's been doing some sleuthing of her own. She's been over at the library, chatting with Rebecca. And it seems she asked Janice Anderson where she got it, and Janice has no memory of ever having seen that lighter before the morning Rebecca bought it."

Oliver groaned. "I suspect Janice can't remember where she got half the merchandise in her store," he said. "And the stuff she was selling at the flea market was just junk. Besides, what about Jules Hartwick? What mysterious item supposedly showed up there?"

"There was a locket," Lois replied. "Celeste found it on the lawn after the snow melted."

"Which means that anyone could have dropped it sometime between December and three weeks ago, when Celeste and Madeline got back from Boston," Oliver pointed out. "I would hardly call that conclusive evidence of anything."

"Hey, don't shoot the messenger," Lois protested. "I'm just reporting what Edna Burnham said."

"She *said* a great deal," Oliver remarked dryly. "But what actually is she getting at? Does she think there's some kind of curse on these things?"

Lois Martin shrugged elaborately. "You said it, not me." She hesitated, but then decided she might as well tell him everything Edna had said. "She also said something about Rebecca having seen someone at the Hartwicks' the night of the party—presumably the someone who left the locket, I suppose. Furthermore, Edna maintains that each and every one of the families who received these objects has some connection to the Asylum. Or at least did have, back when it was open."

"Aha!" Oliver said, as if Lois had finally delivered incontrovertible proof of the ludicrous nature of Edna Burnham's speculations. "Find me a family in Blackstone that *didn't*." Oliver's eyes glittered with challenge. "The Asylum was the mainstay of the economy around here for years. Everyone in town had a relative working there, and half of them had relatives who were *in* the place, for God's sake!"

Lois held up her hands as if to fend off his words. "Hey, I'm not the one you have to convince. It's Edna—" She paused, then grinned with malicious enjoyment. "—and the hundred or so other people she's probably convinced by now."

"Oh, Lord." Oliver groaned again. "What am I supposed to do? Write an article about some ancient evil that's suddenly come forth from the Asylum to wreak havoc on us all?"

"Hey, that's not bad," Lois deadpanned. "I can see the headline now: 'Beware the Blackstone Curse.' "

"How about this one instead," Oliver shot back. " 'Beware the Unemployed Assistant Editor.' "

He was smiling as he turned and headed toward the rear of the building to the renovated office that Bill McGuire had finally finished last week. He busied himself readying the paper for the press, but try as he did to put Edna Burnham's outrageous theory out of his thoughts, Oliver found himself coming back to it over and over again. As the day wore on, and Edna's speculations kept popping unbidden back into his mind, he knew the idea must be churning around other minds in Blackstone as well.

Finally, shortly after noon, with this week's *Chronicle* put to bed but his thoughts still restless, he gave up. "I'm going home," he told Lois. "I might even go up to the Asylum and take a look around." He managed a grin he didn't quite feel. "Who knows? Maybe I'll even find something that will prove Edna's right."

"Better if you can find something that proves she's wrong," Lois replied.

"More likely, I won't find anything at all."

Leaving the office, he thought about stopping into the library to see Rebecca Morrison, then remembered the dark glares he'd received from Germaine Wagner the last few times he'd turned up during working hours. Better to come back at closing time, when Germaine might not approve but at least would have no reason to object if Rebecca chose to let him walk her home.

Walk her home? He sounded like a high school kid. Obviously, the spring fever was back!

As he started up North Hill, Oliver found himself eyeing a few crocuses he might just steal for Rebecca later on in the afternoon. But then, when he came to the gates of the Asylum and stopped to look directly at the building, his good mood vanished.

Just the idea of entering the deserted building was enough to make his stomach cramp, and it wasn't until he had turned away from the Asylum, walked back down the hill and entered his own house that the knot of pain in his belly began to ease. But his restlessness would not be tamed. He paced the living room, wandered into the kitchen, then back, feeling as though he needed to look for something—something that eluded him.

Almost unconsciously, his eyes moved to the ceiling.

Upstairs?

What was there to search for upstairs? There were only the three bedrooms and the bathroom. Nothing unusual to be discovered there.

Still, he found himself mounting the stairs, entering each room and pulling open the doors of the closets in all three bedrooms, looking for . . . what?

He'd been through these closets dozens of times—maybe hundreds—and knew exactly what was in each of them. Old clothes he hadn't wanted to throw away, boxes of Christmas decorations, his luggage. But nothing from the Asylum.

Still, he searched each one a second time, then started back toward the top of the stairs, where he paused and found himself looking up once more.

The attic?

He couldn't remember the last time he'd been up there. But as he regarded the old-fashioned, spring-loaded, pull-down ladder, it occurred to him that if there really were any old records around, they might just be up in the attic. Even if his own father hadn't stored anything up there, some of the earlier superintendents might have.

Getting the step stool from the kitchen, he reached up and jerked the ladder down. The motion sent a shiver through his spine as the old springs squealed and groaned. With a flashlight in hand, he mounted the stairs, opened the trapdoor that was the attic's only access, and climbed up into the space beneath the house's steeply pitched roof.

An old-fashioned push-button light switch was mounted on a support post. When he pressed it, a bare bulb sputtered on, filling the area with a yellowish glow.

No more than five feet away was an oak filing cabinet and two old wooden fruit crates, faded, curling labels barely clinging to their sides. Opening the top drawer of the filing cabinet, he found a stack of leather-bound ledgers, each of them containing a full year of the Asylum's bookkeeping, the entries noted in the kind of precise accountant's handwriting that has all but disappeared since the advent of the computer.

The second drawer contained more of the same, and so did the fourth. The third drawer, either jammed or locked, wouldn't budge.

He shifted his attention to the crates, testing the top of the first one. Free of nails, its surface was slightly warped and took no effort at all to lift away.

Inside the box were two stacks of file folders.

And something else.

Neatly folded on top of one of the stacks was a piece of cloth. Picking it up, Oliver gingerly unfolded it, then took it over to hold it under the light.

It was a handkerchief made of linen, and though he wasn't an expert, it looked as though the lace around its edges was handmade. In addition to the delicate lace edging, a pattern of flowers in colors so pale he could hardly discern them had been embroidered into the material, forming an intricate wreath all around the handkerchief's perimeter and spreading out to encircle an ornate symbol that had been worked into one corner. For a moment Oliver wasn't sure what the symbol was, but then, when he turned the handkerchief over and discovered that the other side was as flawlessly embroidered as the first, he understood.

The symbol was actually two R's worked carefully

back to back, so that each side of the monogrammed handkerchief would be exactly the same.

No right side.

No wrong side.

Refolding the handkerchief, he put it back into the crate, then hefted the wooden box itself and carefully inched his way down the ladder. After going back for the second crate, he closed the trapdoor, folded the ladder back up against the ceiling, then took the boxes into one of the spare bedrooms and began unpacking their contents onto the bed. Just as he'd hoped, they turned out to be old patient files.

For the rest of the afternoon, his fascination growing as he read, Oliver pored over the old files, marveling not only at the strange diagnoses that had been made in the early days of the Asylum but at the cruel treatments that were prescribed.

Bed restraints had been commonplace.

Straitjackets had been ordinary.

Even detailed accounts of ice-water baths and prefrontal lobotomies were recorded with no more emotion than might have been used in lab reports describing the dissection of an insect or the interaction between two chemicals.

His revulsion growing with every page he read, Oliver slowly began to understand his horror of the Asylum, even after all the years that had gone by since it was closed down.

A torture chamber.

That was what it had been. A place of unspeakable sadness and pain.

Even now he could imagine the screams that must have echoed inside the building.

Screams, he suddenly realized, that he surely would have heard when he was a child, living here, in the superintendent's cottage, no more than fifty yards away. Yet he had no memory of them.

But shouldn't he have heard the agonized howls that would have clawed through his open windows on summer nights, ripping into his dreams, turning them into nightmares?

The answer came to him as quickly as had the question: the records he had found were far older than he, Oliver realized, and when his father had taken over the Asylum, the inhumanity must have ended.

The solution brought no satisfaction, however. For if the horrors that had taken place within the Asylum's walls had truly ended when his father became superintendent, then why couldn't he bring himself to go into the building?

Other memories! There must be other memories, too horrible for him to face!

Suddenly unwilling to delve any deeper into the files, Oliver replaced them carefully in the crate. As he did so, he spotted the handkerchief again and picked it up, marveling anew at the perfection of the work, and wondering who had sewn it. Most likely not a patient—such delicate work required skill and concentration hard to imagine in someone mentally disturbed.

Surely, he thought, it must have been made by one of the staff members, filling the endless empty hours of the night shifts.

He held its soft fabric in his fingers, and once more his eye fell on the double-sided R that had been worked so cleverly into one corner.

Instantly he knew what he would do with the handkerchief.

As he found some paper with which to wrap his gift, Oliver imagined the look of delight on the recipient's face as she opened it.

Even if old Edna Burnham was right, he thought, and the gifts that had apparently come from nowhere to the homes of Elizabeth McGuire and Jules Hartwick and

Martha Ward had brought with them some kind of evil, there could be no doubt where *this* gift had come from.

It had come from his own attic, where it had been stored for more years than he could remember.

And Rebecca would love it.

Chapter 2

"*R*ebecca? *Rebecca!* I want you!"

Rebecca Morrison cringed as the querulous voice ricocheted from the floor above, immediately followed by the hollow thumping of a rubber-tipped cane pounding against bare hardwood planks. She had come home from the library early today, sent by Germaine to clean out the cupboards under the sink. She wasn't certain exactly why this chore had to be accomplished today, since it didn't look to her as if anyone had cleaned anything out from under the kitchen sink for at least twenty years, but it was what Germaine wanted her to do, and she knew she owed Germaine a very great deal. Germaine, after all, had explained it to her the day after the fire that had destroyed her aunt's home.

"I hope you understand what a sacrifice Mother and I are making," Germaine had said. She was perched on the edge of the single straight-backed chair that, save for the bed, was the only place to sit in the small attic room that Rebecca had been given. "Except for the cleaning girl, Mother isn't used to having anyone but me in the house. However, if you're very quiet, she might get used to you. We'll have to let the cleaning girl go, of course, but with your extra hands to help us out, I don't think we'll miss her too much, will we?"

Rebecca shook her head, as she knew she was expected to do, and when she spoke, it was in the hushed tone she'd learned to use in the library. "I'll be careful not to disturb Mrs. Wagner at all," she said.

"You mustn't call Mother 'Mrs. Wagner,' " Germaine had instructed her. "After all, you're not the cleaning girl, are you? I think if you call her Miss Clara, that will be fine." Rebecca thought calling a widow who was nearly eighty "Miss" was a little strange, but after having worked for Germaine at the library, she knew better than to argue with her. "We'll be just like a little family, taking care of each other," Germaine said with a sigh of satisfaction, and for a moment Rebecca thought the woman might just reach out and pat her on the knee. Instead, she rose from the chair and, in the tone of a grande dame, added, "It isn't everyone who would have taken you in, Rebecca. You should be very grateful to Mother for allowing you to live here."

"Oh, I am," Rebecca quickly assured her. "And I really like this room, Germaine. I mean, what would I put in the dressers and closets in all the big bedrooms downstairs?"

For some reason, her words seemed to make Germaine angry; Rebecca saw her lips tighten into the thin line she used to silence rowdy children in the library, but then she'd turned and left.

Left alone, Rebecca had unpacked her few belongings. All her clothes and possessions had perished in the fire, but she'd purchased some necessary items, and Bonnie Becker, Ed's wife, had brought over some clothing that morning. ("I won't hear of your refusing me," Bonnie had said to her. "These things are almost brand new and they just don't fit. They'll absolutely perfect on you.") After Rebecca hung up the four blouses, one skirt, and two pairs of jeans, and stowed the meager supply of underwear in the tiny pine chest that squatted beneath the one dormer window in the attic room, she started back downstairs. Clara Wagner's shrill voice stopped her just as she was passing the old woman's open door on the second floor, near the foot of the stairs leading to the attic.

"You will bring me a pot of coffee every morning," the old woman had instructed her from the wheelchair in which she was sitting. "Not so hot it will burn my tongue, but not cold either. Do you understand?"

For the next two weeks, Rebecca had done her best, and finally got it right. But more often than not, satisfying Miss Clara's exacting tastes meant running up and down the stairs at least three times every morning before she and Germaine were finally able to leave for work at the library. During the evenings, and on her days off from the library, she'd been busy catching up on all the housework the cleaning girl never seemed to have gotten around to doing.

Now, her unsuccessful attempt to scrub away the cupboard stains was interrupted by Clara Wagner's voice piercing through the vast reaches of the house. Rebecca stood up, stretched her aching back, and let the rag she'd been using drop back into the sink, which was filled with a mixture of hot water, detergent, and bleach.

Leaving the kitchen, she made her way through the walnut-paneled dining room, then into the immense foyer. The pride of the house, the entry hall rose a majestic three stories, crowned by an immense stained-glass skylight set in the roof above, its sunburst pattern filling the huge space with a rainbow of color. On the second-floor level, a broad mezzanine circled the foyer. At the end of the hall opposite the double front doors rose a sweeping staircase that split halfway up, branching in both directions. Sometime after the house had been built, an elevator had been installed on the left side of the foyer, directly opposite the marble-manteled fireplace that dominated the right side. Rebecca had been cautioned that she was never to use the elevator; it was only to be used by Clara Wagner on her infrequent forays to the first floor of her house. Rebecca caught herself holding her breath every time the old lady pushed the button that set the machinery, hidden somewhere in the attic, to grinding ominously as the ornate brass cage rattled slowly from the first floor to the second, or back down. Someday, Rebecca was certain, the ancient contraption was going to break down. She only hoped that Clara Wagner wasn't in the cage when it happened.

As Rebecca mounted the long flight of stairs, the old woman's cane struck the floor twice more. "Rebecca!"

"I'm coming, Miss Clara," she called. "I'll be there in just a second!" Reaching the second floor, she hurried down the long mezzanine toward the room next to the attic stairs.

"Must you shout?" Clara Wagner demanded as Rebecca stepped through her open door. "I'm not deaf, you know!"

"I'm sorry, Miss Clara," Rebecca apologized. "I was in the kitchen trying to—"

"Do you think I care what you were doing?" Clara demanded. Her wheelchair was drawn up close to the room's fireplace, in which a few embers were glowing brightly. With one clawlike hand she pulled her shawl tighter around her thin shoulders, while she used the other to jab her cane toward a glass that sat on a table no more than two feet away.

"Hand me that glass," she said. "And put some more wood on the fire. It's freezing in here."

"Would you like me to turn the heat up?" Rebecca offered.

Clara glared at her. "Do you have any idea what oil costs these days? No, of course you don't! Why would you? You always had your aunt to take care of you, didn't you?"

"Heating oil costs a dollar a gallon," Rebecca offered.

"Don't you dare mock me, Rebecca Morrison!" the old woman snapped. "You might get away with it with my fool of a daughter, but I won't tolerate it. As long as you're living under my roof, you'll keep a civil tongue in your head!"

Rebecca's face burned with shame. "I'm so sorry, Miss Clara," she began. "I didn't mean to—"

Clara jabbed her sharply with the cane. "Don't tell me what you meant and what you didn't mean! Now, what are you waiting for? Hand me that glass, and do something about that fire. And mind you, don't leave the door open when you bring the wood in! I hate a draft as much as I hate laziness," she added, glaring pointedly at Rebecca.

Rebecca handed her the glass from the table, then hurried out of the room and downstairs. The woodpile was back behind the garage; Germaine had forbidden her to move any of the firewood closer to the laundry room door, where it would have been much handier. "The woodpile has always been behind the garage, Rebecca," Germaine had explained. "And that is where it will stay. Mother doesn't like to see things out of their usual place."

Rebecca, though, was fairly sure that Clara Wagner hadn't been anywhere near the laundry room in years. Except for her brief public appearance at Elizabeth McGuire's funeral, Rebecca doubted the old woman had even been outside the house in years. Well, she certainly wasn't going to argue with either of the women who had been kind enough to take her into their own home. Picking up the leather sling that was the only thing Germaine allowed her to carry wood in, she went out to the backyard, stacked five pieces of wood into the carrier, and returned to Clara's room.

"That's hardly enough to keep me warm for the evening," the old woman observed tartly as Rebecca piled three of the logs onto the fire, then used a bellows to fan the embers back to life.

"I'll bring more later on," Rebecca promised. Glancing at the clock, she saw that it was nearly five. "Right now I have to finish in the kitchen. Germaine wanted the cupboard under the sink clean before she came home today."

"Then I suggest you don't waste any more time chattering," Clara told her. "And I shall have tea this afternoon. In the front parlor. Have it ready at six. And I don't mean ready in the kitchen at six, Rebecca. Have it in the *parlor* at six!"

"Yes, Miss Clara," Rebecca replied, scurrying out of the room.

As she returned to the kitchen, she wondered—not for the first time—if perhaps she'd made a mistake moving in here. But where else could she go? Oliver had offered to take her in—he was so sweet—but Germaine made it clear that such an improper arrangement simply would not do. Even now Rebecca could remember Germaine's words as she'd brought her into the house the night of the fire.

"There aren't many people who would do this for you, Rebecca. So I suggest you make everything as easy for Mother and me as you possibly can."

Since then, Rebecca had been laboring to please Germaine and her mother, and she would continue to. But sometimes it seemed that no matter what she did, it was never quite enough.

As she lowered herself back down to her hands and knees, determined to go after the stain under the sink and vanquish it, Rebecca chastised herself for her ingratitude.

She would just have to try a little harder to please Miss Clara, and everything would be all right.

They would be just like a little family—just the way Germaine had said.

Oliver's timing was almost perfect: he'd added fifteen extra minutes to his estimate of the time it would take him to stroll along the path through the woods to the top of Harvard Street, then down to Main and over to the library. Ten minutes had been added in response to his spring fever, which had noticeably worsened as the weather improved throughout the afternoon. He'd tacked on another five to account for a few minutes to survey again the ruins of Martha Ward's house: he was still trying to fathom the twists of psychosis that had led to that strange night a month ago when Martha had burned the place down around herself while she prayed in the flickering light of her votive candles, surrounded by her beloved religious icons. The fire chief determined that the blaze had been deliberate, but no one had yet found any trace of the dragon-shaped cigarette lighter, although Rebecca guessed that they'd find it in the ashes that were all that remained of her aunt's chapel. While he'd said nothing to Rebecca, Oliver privately suspected that someone—perhaps one of the volunteer firemen—had indeed found it, and simply pocketed it as a macabre souvenir of that terrible night. Still, after circling the blackened pit where the house had once stood, he'd poked among the ashes for a minute or so on the off chance that he might stumble upon it.

He hadn't.

Now, at precisely five minutes before the library was due to close, he jogged up the steps and pushed through the double set of doors. As usual, Germaine Wagner glanced up as Oliver entered her domain; also as usual, her expression hardened into a thin-lipped grimace as she recognized him. Since Rebecca had moved into the Wagners' house, Oliver had decided, Germaine's disapproval of him had grown stronger than ever. When a quick glance around didn't reveal Rebecca, he forced himself to give Germaine a friendly smile and approached the counter.

"Is Rebecca around?" he asked, hoping to seem casual, though he did not feel at all nonchalant.

"No," Germaine replied. For a moment there was an impasse as the editor and the librarian gazed at each other, neither of them willing to impart any more information than absolutely necessary.

Oliver broke first. "She isn't sick, is she? Did she come to work?"

Germaine Wagner seemed to weigh the possibility of getting him to leave without pressing her with endless questions but quickly decided the chances were close to nil. "Rebecca's fine," she reported. "She simply left early today. There were some chores at home she needed to complete."

Needed to complete? She made it sound as though Rebecca was late with her homework, Oliver thought. He wondered if Germaine used the same patronizing tone when she talked directly to Rebecca as she invariably did when she talked *about* her, and whether it annoyed Rebecca as much as it did him. But of course it wouldn't—it was exactly the sort of trait Rebecca always managed not to notice in people, let alone find offensive.

Not for the first time, Oliver reflected that if Martha Ward had really been as interested in saints as she claimed to be, she should have been able to recognize that she had one living in her own house. Martha Ward, though, had been just as condescending to Rebecca as Germaine Wagner was.

"Well, maybe I'll just stop over and say hello," he said, deliberately keeping his gaze steadily on Germaine, waiting to see if she would object. This time it was she who broke, turning brusquely back to her work, but gripping her pencil so hard Oliver could see her knuckles turning white.

As he left the library, Oliver wondered once again exactly what Germaine Wagner's problem really was. Was it him? Rebecca? Both of them? But as he emerged back into the warmth of the late afternoon, he decided he didn't really care—it was far too nice an April day to waste much energy on worrying about Germaine Wagner.

Walking up Princeton Street, he crossed Maple, then turned right on Elm. It was just a few minutes after five o'clock when he raised the knocker on the front door of Clara Wagner's house. Rapping it twice, he waited a moment, then pressed the button next to the door. Before the chimes had quite died away, Rebecca opened the door. The questioning look in her eyes as she pulled the door open instantly gave way to a warm smile. The smile disappeared as quickly as it had come, as Clara Wagner's voice called down from above.

"Rebecca? Who is it? Who's at the door?"

Rebecca glanced anxiously over her shoulder. As she hesitated, it occurred to Oliver that she was going to close the door in his face. But then she opened it farther, quickly pulled him inside, and, maneuvering around him, shut the door.

"It's Oliver, Miss Clara," she called to the upper reaches of the house. "Oliver Metcalf!"

Oliver stepped farther into the foyer. From this vantage point he could see Germaine's mother. Sitting in her wheelchair, a shawl clutched tightly around her shoulders, she was glaring down from the mezzanine.

"What does he want? And don't shout, Rebecca. I'm not deaf, you know!"

"Hello, Mrs. Wagner," Oliver said, nodding to her. "Isn't it a lovely day?"

It was as if he hadn't spoken. "I'm going to need more firewood, Rebecca," Clara Wagner said. "My room is no warmer than it was an hour ago!" Turning her chair away from the balustrade, she wheeled herself back into her room. Oliver and Rebecca heard her door close with an angry thud.

"Is she always that charming?" Oliver asked.

Rebecca's eyes clouded slightly. "She's old, and she doesn't get out very much, and—"

"And she can still be polite," Oliver cut in, but as Rebecca flinched at his words, he wished he could take

Most of all, Germaine.

The years had ground slowly by as Germaine waited on her invalid mother. She prepared her meals and kept her bathed. At first, when she'd still believed that Clara would either recover or quickly die, she tried to keep her entertained as well. She'd gotten her to movies and concerts, even taken her on trips. But it had never been good enough. There was something wrong with everything they did and every place they went. After a while, when it became clear that Clara was neither on the verge of recovery nor hovering on the doorstep of death, Germaine had given up. It was no longer worth the effort to try to cajole and plead and lift and push her mother into activities that Clara showed no sign of appreciating. Her father had left just enough money to keep up the house, and Germaine's paycheck, while not generous, yielded just enough for her to hire a part-time cleaning girl, giving her at least a partial respite from her mother's complaints each day.

But every day when Germaine came home from the library, Clara demanded to know what she had brought her, like a spoiled child asking for candy.

Well, today she had something to offer, even if it was only the little gift that Oliver Metcalf had given to Rebecca.

She would have to do something about that situation. When the idea of inviting Rebecca to live with her had come to her in a flash of inspiration as she watched Martha Ward's house burn to the ground, it hadn't occurred to her that Oliver Metcalf might be a problem. Indeed, it had seemed to Germaine that Rebecca would be the perfect solution for her. She would take Rebecca in, and a grateful Rebecca could take over not only the duties of the cleaning girl—thus allowing her to save a dollar or two—but much of the care of her mother as well.

It also hadn't occurred to her how quickly she would

become annoyed by everything about Rebecca. The girl never complained about anything, and always seemed able to find the good in everything. As far as Germaine was concerned, that made her a fool.

But it was Oliver Metcalf who bothered her more. He was starting to hang around—a situation that could lead to no good at all in Germaine's estimation. Well, she would simply forbid Rebecca to see him anymore, and that would be that. At least Rebecca—unlike her mother—would do as she told her to do.

"Germaine? Is that you?"

She flinched as her mother's voice jabbed into her reverie as sharply as needles stuck into flesh. "Yes, Mother," she said, finally stepping through the doorway to face the old woman.

Clara's hooded eyes fixed on her. "What were you doing out there? Were you spying on me?"

Germaine cast around in her mind for an excuse for having lingered outside the door, but knew there was none that would satisfy her mother. "I wasn't doing anything," she finally admitted.

"You were spying on me," Clara accused.

"For heaven's sake, Mother, why would I do that?" Too late, Germaine realized she'd let her exasperation be revealed by her voice.

"Don't use that tone on me, young lady," Clara snapped. "I'm your mother, and you'll show proper respect." Her eyes narrowed suspiciously. "You didn't bring me anything today, did you?"

"You're wrong," Germaine said. "I brought you something wonderful today. Look!" Crossing to the wheelchair, Germaine knelt and placed the handkerchief in her mother's lap.

Clara stared at the handkerchief for a long moment, then her gaze shifted and the bright black eyes fixed sharply on Germaine.

"Where?" she asked. "Where did you get this?"

Germaine's jaw tightened in anger. Was that all her mother cared about? Where it had come from? Next she would be demanding to know how much she'd paid for it. Well, if that was all that counted, fine! "I found it in Janice Anderson's shop," she said.

"Liar!" Clara rasped. Then, with no warning at all, she spat in her daughter's face.

As Germaine fled from the room, Clara's voice rose in a furious howl that pursued her down the stairs. "Liar! *Liar! LIAR!*"

Chapter 3

Oliver Metcalf wasn't sure exactly what it was about the file that caught his eye. He hadn't really been thinking about what he was doing; indeed, more of his attention had been focused on his growing concern about Germaine Wagner's influence over Rebecca Morrison than on the task of packing the old files he'd brought down from the attic back into their box. Yet the moment he'd picked up the faded folder he was now holding, he knew there was something different about it.

The folder itself was made of the same buff manila paper as all the others, mottled with age, its edges softened and fraying. The tab on the edge showed a discoloration where the identifying sticker had once been glued, but the label had long ago fallen away.

Dropping onto the straight-backed chair that he had positioned next to the guest room's single window, Oliver opened the file. As he scanned its first page, he felt the pangs of a headache coming on. Absently, he rubbed his fingers against his temple, as if hoping to massage the pain away before it took root, and focused on the handwritten notes.

The first page bore nothing more than the patient's vital statistics. Her name—Lavinia Willoughby—meant nothing to Oliver, and her home had been someplace in South Carolina called Devereaux. Complaining of depression, she had been brought to the Asylum by her husband, and was admitted in 1948.

According to the record, she had died in the Asylum four years later.

The year Oliver was born.

As he began reading Lavinia Willoughby's case history, Oliver unconsciously pressed the fingers of his right hand harder against his temple, which was starting to throb with pain. Mrs. Willoughby was diagnosed as manic-depressive, and the treatment prescribed for her had been typical of her time. There had been some counseling, with a great deal of emphasis put on her relationship with her father. As her counseling progressed, it became clear that Lavinia's doctor had concluded that there had been an incestuous relationship between Lavinia and her father.

Lavinia Willoughby, though, had apparently not agreed with the doctor, for there was a notation on the same page that the patient was "in denial and refusing to deal with the possibility."

A few pages further on, the doctor began exploring the suggestion that Lavinia herself had initiated the incestuous relationship, though it was duly noted that the patient also denied that possibility. After that session, the doctor prescribed hydrotherapy for his patient.

Oliver's headache spread from his right temple to the back of his head as he read the account of Lavinia Willoughby's three sessions in the hydrotherapy room. The first one had lasted an hour, after which the patient developed "pneumonia unrelated to her therapy session." When she had recovered from her illness, her therapy resumed, and after the third session, in which she'd been immersed in cold water for three hours, her therapy had proved successful. The next day, in her regular counseling session, Lavinia Willoughby had remembered that her father had, indeed, molested her when she was a small child.

Looking up from the file as the afternoon light began to fade, Oliver's eyes moved to the looming form of the

Asylum atop the hill. Its gray walls seemed almost prison-like this afternoon, and though neither the room nor the day was cold, Oliver found himself shivering as he imagined what incarceration there must have been like for Lavinia Willoughby. He scanned the blank and filthy windows of the ancient stone building, wondering which of them might have been Lavinia Willoughby's, which of those barred portals might have stood between her and the world outside the Asylum's walls.

How had she stood it? How had any of them stood it? Even if they weren't insane when they entered that building, surely they would have been after only a few months' stay.

His headache spreading into his left temple now, Oliver switched on the lamp that was on the table between the bed and the chair in which he sat, and went back to Lavinia Willoughby's file.

It was after her acknowledgment of her relationship with her father—and her admission that she had initiated it—that electroconvulsive therapy had been prescribed for Lavinia.

As Oliver began reading the description of the treatment that had been administered to her, a blinding stab of pain slashed through his head and a shroud of utter blackness closed around him.

The boy is looking straight up, watching the pattern of light and shadow on the ceiling change. He knows it is useless to struggle against the thick leather straps that hold him to the gurney: even if he could work his arms and legs free, there is no place to run to, for he knows there is no way to escape the people who have tied him down, let alone escape the building itself.

He tries not to think about where they might be taking him, but it doesn't matter.

All of the rooms are the same.

All of them terrify him.

The gurney stops, and the boy is able to shift his eyes just enough to see a door. A plaque is mounted on it, with three letters:

E. C. T.

The boy doesn't know what the letters mean, but he instantly knows that all the rooms are not the same and this is the worst of all of them.

He can feel a scream building in his throat, but he struggles against it, knowing if he shows how terrified he is, it will only be worse. Besides, even if anyone heard him scream, they wouldn't come to help him.

They never do.

One of the orderlies opens the door, and the other one pushes the gurney inside. The boy catches a glimpse of the box on a table against one of the walls, and feels the knot in his stomach turn into a ball of fire.

And suddenly he has to go to the bathroom.

He tries to tell the orderly, but now he is so terrified that his mouth has gone dry, and the only sound that comes out is a choking sob as he struggles not to cry.

He shuts his eyes: maybe if he doesn't watch, it won't happen.

When he hears the door open and close, and the familiar voice ask if everything is ready, he squeezes his eyes shut tighter, as if by closing out more of the light he might close out the sound of the voice as well.

The darkness, though, is even more frightening than what he has seen, and when he finally risks a peek, he knows it is going to happen again.

The wooden box is open, and the man is taking the bright metal plates out of it.

Though the boy tries not to watch, he can't help himself, and his eyes never leave the metal contacts as the man applies a gooey substance to them, then snaps them into a heavy band of rubber.

One of the orderlies fastens the band around the boy's head.

As the boy braces himself, the orderlies bend over him, pressing his body down against the gurney. He squeezes his eyes shut again.

The first shock jolts through him, and every muscle in his body convulses, jerking his limbs against the restraining straps with so much force he thinks his legs and arms must be broken.

But even worse is the hot wetness spreading from his crotch and the stink coming from behind his buttocks.

Crying as much from shame as from the pain, the boy waits for the next shock.

And the next.

And the next . . .

Melissa Holloway exited the front door of the bank just as Ed Becker's Buick pulled up to the curb.

"See how prompt I am?" Bill McGuire got out of the passenger seat and held the door for Melissa. "Give me a schedule, and I adhere to it."

Though his inflection was bantering, the nervous look in the contractor's eyes belied his tone, and as Melissa waved him into the front seat while she herself got into the back of the big sedan, she tried to allay his obvious fears.

"This is only a formality, Bill," she said. "I just think I ought to at least take one good look at the project, since suddenly it's going to be *my* name signing off on the final approval for the loan."

"Yours, and the board's," Ed Becker reminded her.

"Mine and the board's," Melissa agreed. "But why don't I think it's the board that's going to get fired if anything goes wrong?"

"Nothing's going to go wrong," Bill McGuire assured her as Ed turned up Amherst Street. "Jules was all set to fund the loan when—"

"Jules isn't here anymore," Melissa cut in, deciding it was time for her to assert herself a little more strongly. "And let's not forget that we're not quite out of the woods on the audit yet. If the loan has to hinge solely on Jules's last recommendation, I'm afraid it's not going to fly." She saw the two men in the front seat glance uneasily at each other, but neither of them said anything. "Let's also not forget that it was the way Jules ran the bank that got us into trouble in the first place."

"But the Center Project is perfectly sound—" Bill McGuire began. This time it was Ed Becker who cut him off.

"Melissa knows the math better than either one of us," the lawyer told him. "She knows it works on paper. But a good banker wants to know it's going to work in the real world too."

"I know." Bill sighed. "It's just that ever since this whole thing began ... well, you both know what I'm saying."

Though neither Ed Becker nor Melissa Holloway replied, they did, indeed, know exactly what Bill was saying. For the last four months, ever since Bill's wife had miscarried their second child, only to kill herself a few days later, a sense of foreboding had fallen over the town. When the news had spread that there were problems at the bank, and then Jules Hartwick disemboweled himself on the steps of the Asylum, the foreboding had turned to apprehension. No one, though, had expected

Martha Ward to be next. Her fiery death ignited a conflagration of fear and suspicion in Blackstone. The very atmosphere throbbed with anxiety. Neighbors who for years had greeted each other with cheerful hellos had now begun to cast wary eyes on their fellow townsmen, as if trying to ferret out who might next fall victim to whatever curse had been visited upon the town.

And each of them prayed that he might be spared.

Their arrival at the Asylum did nothing to dispel the mood that had descended over all three of them. As Melissa Holloway got out of the Buick's backseat and gazed up at the building's grimy stone facade, an unbidden vision of the hospital in which she herself had once been confined came into her mind, and she wondered if she really wanted to venture through the great oaken doors. But as Bill McGuire turned the key in the lock and the heavy door creaked open, Melissa firmly put her memories aside, reminding herself that what had happened in Secret Cove when she was a child had nothing to do with Blackstone today. Taking a deep breath—a breath that almost succeeded in calming her nerves— she followed Ed Becker and Bill McGuire as they led the way into the Asylum.

Little was left of the splendor that had graced the building in the days before it had been converted from a private mansion into a hospital for the insane. What had once been a series of large, elegant rooms had at some point been subdivided into a warren of tiny offices. Bill McGuire led them from room to room explaining the building's original floor plan and describing what it would look like when the reconstruction was completed. "This will become an atrium," he said as they returned to the entry hall. As they threaded their way through the maze of empty rooms on the west side of the building, the fading sunlight that filtered through the dirt-encrusted windows did little to dispel the ominousness of the place. Finally, toward the rear of the building, they came to the foot of what once must have been an impressive staircase.

"The stairs are original," Bill pointed out, "but somewhere along the line the mahogany banisters and balustrades were replaced with metal ones. Probably at the same time the sprinkler system was put in." He gazed sourly up at the network of pipes suspended from a Celotex ceiling of the kind that had been popular back in the late forties and early fifties. "The last remodeling was done only a couple of years before they closed the place."

"Why *did* they close it?" Melissa asked.

Bill McGuire and Ed Becker exchanged glances. In the silence that followed, each of them seemed to be waiting for the other to speak. It was Ed who finally said, "No one really knows exactly what happened." He paused. "Oliver Metcalf's father was the superintendent, and when Oliver and his twin sister were almost four, his sister died. There were all kinds of rumors at the time. Most people thought it was an accident, but some people blamed Oliver. There were even a few who blamed Dr. Metcalf. It was before my time, of course, but local lore has it that things went downhill from there. Metcalf never really recovered from the tragedy. Over time, many of the patients were moved to other places, and there weren't any new ones. In the end, when Metcalf died, the trustees decided to shut it down instead of trying to find a new director."

"So the building just sat empty for forty years?" Melissa asked. "What a waste."

"On the other hand, at least they didn't tear it down," Bill McGuire said. He had started up the stairs and motioned for them to follow. "There's still enough left that it can be restored and expanded." As he led them up to the second floor, he explained how the reconstruction would be done, first by restoring the original entry hall and returning both the second and third floors to the galleries they had once been. "The bedrooms up here were huge, but they got chopped up into cubicles just like the rooms on the ground floor. They'll make terrific shops, and down on the first floor, the kitchen's still almost up to commercial standards. We've found enough pictures of the original dining room that we can restore it almost perfectly."

As the light continued to drain away, Bill McGuire flipped on the flashlight he'd brought along. Moving steadily through the rooms on the second floor, he carefully explained to Melissa the plans for every area, and what kind of shops had already agreed to lease space. Then, on the third floor, they discovered some rooms that weren't quite empty. In one of the old patients' rooms there was still a Formica-topped table and a chair; in another they discovered an old oak dresser. Its finish was nearly gone and its top surface slightly warped, but its frame was still solid, its brass fittings and pulls still intact though blackened with age.

Ed Becker pulled one of the curved drawers out of the dresser and took it to the window, where enough light was still leaking through for him to examine the dovetail joinery that a craftsman had used to fit the corners together. Though the light was nearly gone, he could see that the joinery had all been done by hand, and that its gracefully curved expanse had been carved from a single block of wood, not fitted together from pieces.

"What are you going to do with this?" he asked.

Bill McGuire shrugged.

"Any chance of buying it?"

"You'd do better to ask Melissa than me," Bill said.

"What was done with the rest of the furniture?" the young banker asked.

"I had Corelli Brothers come and haul it out a few months ago. It was all auctioned off, and the money was put into the Center account. They must have just missed a few things up here."

Melissa's brow furrowed. "Well, there's not enough left to be worth an auctioneer's time. What do you think it's worth?" Ed Becker eyed the dresser, calculating how much of an underestimation of its value he might get away with, but Melissa seemed to read his mind. "Given that it's hand-carved, I don't see that it would go for much less than a thousand at auction, do you, Bill?"

"I think she's on to you, Ed," the contractor said, grinning. "But look at it this way—by the time you finish restoring it, it'll be worth twice that."

Ed Becker's eyes moved over the dresser, appraising its workmanship again. Though he and Bonnie couldn't afford quite that much right now, he knew the chest was worth at least the thousand Melissa had suggested. Moreover, there was something about it—something he couldn't quite put his finger on—that made him feel he had to own it. It was a beauty, after all.

Whatever the reason, he wanted the dresser. "No slack, huh?" he asked.

Melissa and Bill shook their heads. "You'll have to clear the purchase with the rest of the Center's board of directors," she told him, a smile playing over her face. "They might claim you have a conflict of interest."

Ed Becker rolled his eyes. "They'll be so happy to get a thousand dollars out of me, they won't argue for a second." Putting the drawer back in the dresser, he moved to follow Bill McGuire and Melissa Holloway out of the room, but turned back at the doorway to look at the old piece of furniture one more time.

Even at a thousand dollars, he decided, it was still a hell of a deal. From the zippered portfolio he was carrying, he extracted a legal pad and pen and wrote in bold capitals: PROPERTY OF ED BECKER. DO NOT REMOVE. And folding the paper so it would hang from the drawer when closed, he staked his claim.

But as he turned away from the chest once more, he

felt a sudden chill, as if he'd been struck by a draft from an open window.

He glanced around the room again, but the window was closed tight and none of the panes was even cracked, let alone broken.

As he hurried to catch up with Bill and Melissa, he dismissed the strange chill, telling himself it must have been nothing more than his imagination.

Chapter 4

Clara Wagner gazed down at the handkerchief that still lay in her lap, exactly where Germaine had left it. Since her daughter had left the room half an hour before, Clara hadn't moved at all. The fire on the hearth had burned low, but for once she hadn't called out, hadn't banged her cane on the floor to bring Germaine or Rebecca running to do her bidding.

For half an hour she'd done nothing at all except sit in her chair, gazing at the handkerchief.

Why did it look so familiar to her?

And why did the very sight of it so frighten her?

Somewhere deep in the recesses of her mind, this small scrap of linen with its elaborate floral design had stirred a memory, but no matter how she tried, she couldn't quite grasp it, couldn't get it quite close enough to pull into the light. Annoyingly—maddeningly—its significance hovered in the blurry fringes of her memory, refusing to come into focus.

Was it possible that Germaine hadn't been lying, and that she'd actually found the handkerchief in Janice Anderson's antique shop?

She supposed it was barely possible, though she'd never admit as much to Germaine. A strong and certain sense within told her she had seen this handkerchief before. And it came from no shop.

The handkerchief had stirred her memory the moment she laid eyes on it. And not a pleasant memory either.

Her stomach—delicate even when she was feeling at her best—had instantly churned, and bile boiled up into her throat, leaving a sour taste in her mouth. For a moment she'd even thought she might vomit. She hadn't, of course; instead she'd sat motionless, willing her body to respond to her wishes, just as she'd willed it to respond when she decided she no longer wished to walk. That memory still made her smile, for when Germaine had brought Dr. Margolis to see her, he hadn't been able even to find a reflex in the legs she'd decided never again to use. Philip Margolis—and a host of neurologists and orthopedists to whom Germaine had dragged her—agreed that she couldn't walk. None of them could determine the cause. The wheelchair—and Germaine—had become her legs.

Precisely as she'd intended.

Ever since that day eighteen years ago, Clara had felt completely in control of everything about her life. Her daughter did her bidding, and her cleaning girl did her bidding.

Now Rebecca Morrison too did her bidding.

But for some reason—a reason she couldn't quite fathom—the handkerchief was upsetting her. Picking it up as gingerly as if it could have burned her, she held it under her reading light, examining it more closely.

It had indeed been skillfully done, every loop and knot of the tatting perfectly even, every tiny stitch of embroidery executed with such remarkable precision that she could find neither a knot nor a tag end of the fine silk thread showing anywhere.

Suddenly an image from the past flashed through her mind. An image of a woman, clad in nothing more than a thin cotton nightgown, sitting on the edge of a metal-framed bed, gazing straight ahead, seemingly at nothing.

But in her lap, her fingers were working so quickly they were little more than a blur as she wove silken thread into a square of fine linen.

Clara's fingers tightened on the handkerchief. But of course the idea that was forming in her mind was impossible. More than half a century had passed since Clara had so much as set foot in that building! Whatever that woman had been working on had disappeared as utterly as had the woman herself.

Despite her own logic, Clara examined the handkerchief yet again, unable to take her eyes from it, searching for . . . what?

Something that—once again—she couldn't quite grasp. As her memory refused to respond to her demands, and the recollection she sought remained hidden in the shadows, her frustration grew. For a moment she was tempted to hurl the handkerchief into the fireplace. She crumpled it in her hands, squeezing it hard, as if she might be able to wring the memory from its folds, then drew her hand back in preparation for tossing it into the dying flames. At the last second she changed her mind.

She wouldn't destroy the handkerchief—yet.

First she would remember.

Then she would burn it.

As the clock on the mantel above the fireplace struck six, she shoved the handkerchief deep into the pocket of her dress, then placed her right hand on the wheelchair's control panel. With a nearly inaudible hum, the wheelchair rolled out of the room onto the mezzanine.

"For heaven's sake, Rebecca, can't you be more careful? If you drop it, Mother will kill you."

Rebecca tightened her grip on the silver tray bearing the teapot, three cups and saucers, a pitcher of cream, a sugar bowl, a basket of scones, and a box of candy. Germaine had been insistent that she couldn't use the tea cart in the butler's pantry—she must carry the tray in herself, and she mustn't let even a single drop of either the tea or the cream spill. Still, Rebecca knew she had steady hands, and Germaine's reluctance to let her use the cart was no more strange than her demands regarding the preparation of the tea, which she insisted on tasting and had made Rebecca prepare no fewer than four times before declaring that it was satisfactorily brewed.

As she followed Germaine out of the kitchen and through the dining room to the foyer, Rebecca took tiny, careful steps so the surface of the cream barely even moved, let alone threatened to slop over onto the tray. She stopped just outside the dining room door, just as Germaine had instructed. A clanking, followed immediately by the sound of the machinery in the attic coming alive, announced Clara Wagner's imminent arrival. As she and Germaine waited side by side, the brass elevator slowly descended from the mezzanine to the first floor, its door opened, and Clara, her small frame sitting absolutely erect in her wheelchair, emerged from the metal cage. Her eyes fixed balefully on Germaine and Rebecca, almost as if she was sorry they were waiting for her. Rolling the wheelchair across the enormous Oriental carpet that covered all but the edges of the entry hall's walnut floor, Clara inspected the tray. Rebecca could almost feel her searching for something to complain about, and it took her only a moment to find it.

"The sugar bowl isn't full," she announced at the exact second she lifted its lid.

"I'm sorry, Miss Clara," Rebecca said, her face reddening. Why hadn't Germaine told her to fill it? "I'll fill it right away."

"You won't," Clara Wagner declared. "Germaine will do it while you set the tea table."

Rebecca saw a vein in Germaine's forehead throbbing, but she said nothing as Germaine picked the offending sugar bowl off the tray and retreated back toward the kitchen. Rebecca herself followed Clara Wagner as she led the way to the front parlor, where a tea table waited, which Rebecca had already set with three places. Clara eyed them suspiciously, but Rebecca had been careful to get each utensil straight. The damask napkins were folded perfectly. She held her breath as Clara's eyes moved from the china to the jam pots to the butter dish, but those too seemed to meet her standards.

"You may set the tray down," she decreed.

They waited in silence until Germaine arrived with the sugar bowl. Rebecca carefully fixed its level in her mind, determined not to make the same mistake again.

Germaine poured the first cup of tea and set it in front of her mother. "Why don't you show Rebecca the hand-kerchief I gave you?" she asked, her eyes flicking toward Rebecca as if to see if the younger woman would contradict her.

She *did* give it to her mother, Rebecca reminded herself. Oliver gave it to me, but it was Germaine who gave it to Miss Clara. "Thank you," she said as Germaine finally passed her a cup of tea. Then she turned to Clara. "I'd love to see the handkerchief."

Clara Wagner's hand moved automatically to the pocket into which she'd stuffed the handkerchief. "I didn't bring it downstairs," she said. "I don't like it."

The vein in Germaine's forehead began throbbing again as she saw the lump in her mother's pocket and instantly understood what it was. Still stinging from her humiliation over the sugar bowl, she glared at her mother. "If you don't like it, why don't you give it back to me?"

Clara's eyes met her daughter's. "I don't have it," she insisted.

"You do," Germaine replied coldly. She reached over to take the handkerchief out of her mother's pocket, but Clara's fingers closed on her wrist. For a long moment mother and daughter glared at each other. "Are you going to call me a liar again, Mother?" Germaine asked.

Suddenly Clara's hand released Germaine's wrist and

she pulled the handkerchief out of her pocket. "Very well," she said, her voice rasping. "If you want it that badly, have it! Have it with my blessing!" Crushing the handkerchief into a wad, she hurled it in her daughter's face.

Rebecca held her breath, bracing herself for the scene she was certain was about to ensue, but to her relief, Germaine didn't respond to her mother's fury. She merely retrieved the handkerchief from the floor where it had fallen, spread it flat on the table, then folded it carefully. She slipped it into the breast pocket of her blouse so the mirrored R showed perfectly. "There," she said, her eyes fixing once more on Rebecca. "Isn't it pretty?"

Without waiting for an answer, Germaine lifted the lid off the box of chocolates. To her horror, she found no candy inside. Instead of the array of chocolates she'd been expecting, she saw nothing but a pulsating mass of ants, gnats, and flies. Her eyes widened in terror as a cloud of insects swarmed up from the box, flying directly at her face. Screaming, Germaine leaped up from her chair, overturning it in her haste to escape the horde of insects still pouring from the open box. Instinctively, she lashed out at the teeming mass, trying to fend it off, and succeeded only in overturning the teapot. As scalding tea gushed across the table and into Clara's lap, Germaine backed away from the table, but her terror only increased as she spotted the tangle of snakes writhing on the floor around her feet.

Another scream emerged from her throat, and she fled, sobbing and stumbling, from the room.

Rebecca, stunned by Germaine's sudden, unexplained outburst, was frozen in her chair until Clara Wagner's voice penetrated her shock and she realized that the old woman was shouting at her, "Help me! Help me!"

Her dazed confusion broken, Rebecca jumped up and began blotting at Clara Wagner's skirt with a napkin. Her mind was groping for some explanation, but all she could think of was that suddenly, in no more than the blink of an eye, Germaine had gone crazy. But that was impossible, wasn't it?

"What was it?" she asked. "What happened?"

Irritably brushing Rebecca away, Clara Wagner picked up another napkin and started working on her skirt herself. "What does it matter?" she asked. "She's ruined my tea." Without another word, Clara backed away from the table and left the parlor.

Oliver's head snapped up as the file slipped from his lap to the floor, and he bent down to pick it up. His headache was finally loosening its grip, but his whole body hurt, as if he'd just put himself through a punishing workout. His skin was covered with a cold sheen of sweat, and he felt utterly exhausted. It was only as he bent to gather the contents of the file together again that he glanced out the window and noticed that the last of the daylight had slipped away.

Darkness and shadows had enshrouded Blackstone, and the Asylum, looming at the top of the hill, cast the darkest shadow of all. As he gazed at the silhouette of the structure for which his father had been the final overseer, Oliver tried to imagine Malcolm Metcalf committing the kind of atrocities that had been so coldly and clinically described in the case history he now held in his hand.

He could not make himself believe it, despite the conclusive evidence in the pages he had just read—pages of precise notations in his father's own distinctive handwriting.

Accept it, he told himself, accept that the treatments he had prescribed for that patient were far from uncommon back then; indeed, they were considered the most advanced thinking in the treatment of mental illness. Why, then, shouldn't his father have used them?

His thoughts were interrupted by a flash of light from

the top of the hill. Oliver froze, but then decided it had been an illusion.

He saw another flash of light—barely more than a flicker—illuminating one of the third-floor windows for a second, only to disappear as quickly as had the first.

A moment later he saw it again, and then again.

For the tiniest fraction of a second reason completely deserted him and he felt an absolute certainty that he knew who was walking in the Asylum this night.

It was his father.

His father, somehow come back to prowl the darkened corridors of his long-silent domain while he himself read of the sadistic "treatments" in which Malcolm Metcalf had once indulged.

But as quickly as the terrifying sensation came over him, it drained away, and he realized the truth.

He was seeing nothing more than the beam of a flashlight as someone explored the Asylum's empty rooms. Peering out the window, he spotted the dim shape of a car parked close by the Asylum's entrance, and then remembered that this was the day Bill McGuire and Ed Becker were going to take Melissa Holloway through the building.

Straightening the file and putting it back in the box with the others, Oliver went downstairs, took a light jacket from a hook by the front door, and went out into the gathering night. Even if he couldn't bring himself to go into the Asylum, he could certainly wait on the steps for his friends to emerge. But as he started up the slope toward the dark stone structure, he began to feel the familiar throbbing in his right temple.

With every step the pain grew worse, but Oliver kept moving doggedly onward, refusing to give in to the agony in his head. As he reached the bottom step of the short flight leading to the Asylum's front door, a wave of nausea rose in his stomach and he lurched to a stop, dropping to his knees as he felt a clammy sweat break out over his entire body.

Nausea twisted at his guts. Oliver struggled to breathe, then staggered back to his feet. He gazed up at the double oaken doors at the top of the steps. They seemed to grow before his very eyes, doubling in size, then quadrupling. A gurgle of terror bubbling in his throat, Oliver recoiled backward as the great doors began to tip toward him, and he knew that if he stayed where he was even a second longer, he would surely be crushed. Fighting the keening scream that was about to explode from his throat, he turned and fled into the darkness.

Melissa Holloway hesitated at the top of the stairs leading to the Asylum's basement. A shiver passed through her and she felt an odd sense of being suddenly close to some incomprehensible evil.

"We don't have to go down there," Bill McGuire offered, sensing her discomfort. "If you'd rather—"

"It's all right," Melissa quickly cut in. "I came here to see the building, and I'd like to see it all." But as she gazed down at the black pool into which the steps led, she wondered if she really did want to see what was down there. A moment later, though, as the flashlights Ed Becker and Bill McGuire were carrying washed enough of the darkness away to reveal nothing more threatening than what appeared to be a perfectly ordinary corridor, her fears eased. Yet as she followed the two men down the stairs, their footsteps echoing hollowly, her sense of an evil presence grew stronger.

"Are you sure there's no one here but us?" she asked, and immediately regretting her question, reproached herself for sounding like a skittish girl.

"You never really know, do you?" Ed Becker suggested, playfully picking up on her nervousness. "Who

knows what evil once roamed these . . ." His words died
away as Bill McGuire cast the beam of his light into one
of the rooms that opened off the corridor and they saw
the shackles hanging from its walls. "Jesus," the lawyer
whispered. "You don't think they actually used those
things on people, do you?"

Melissa Holloway stared at the thick leather cuffs that
hung from the ends of heavy chains bolted to the wall.
"Can you think of another purpose for them?"

Neither of the men made a reply, but Bill McGuire
shifted his light quickly back to the corridor.

The next two doors were both pierced with small windows, and when Bill McGuire opened one of them,
Melissa and Ed Becker both knew why.

Little more than cells, there were still remnants of
padding hanging from their walls.

There was no furniture.

The three of them gazed wordlessly at the room for a
moment, then moved on.

The room next to the padded cell was equipped with
three large porcelain tubs, each of them big enough for
an adult to stretch out in. All three had heavy wooden
covers. The covers were notched at one end. Ed Becker
stared at them, puzzled.

Again, it was as if Melissa Holloway read his mind.
"For the patients' heads," she said softly. "No one stays
in a tub of cold water voluntarily. So they used covers to
hold them in."

Ed Becker stared open-mouthed at the tubs and tried to
imagine what it would be like to be closed into one of
them. The cold water would be horrible; the immobility
and helplessness even worse. Shuddering, he turned
away. "What the hell kind of place was this?" he mut-
tered as he moved quickly back into the hall.

"No different from hundreds of others, I suspect,"
Melissa Holloway replied.

The three of them finished their tour of the basement in

silence, as if compelled to investigate every one of the dank rooms, all of them used for purposes that none of them really wanted to talk about.

As they finally turned back toward the stairs, Melissa shook her head sadly. "I wonder if we're really doing the right thing," she said, remembering not only the rooms they had just inspected but the ones upstairs as well. "Maybe it would be better just to tear the whole place down."

Bill McGuire and Ed Becker glanced at each other. "Too late for that," the lawyer replied. "The structure's sound. Besides, if it was going to be torn down, it should have been done a long time ago." A grim smile played over his lips. "I know it's spooky, Melissa—frankly, I'm a bit spooked by it myself—but whatever went on here happened so long ago that practically everyone's forgotten about it. All it is now is an historical building. In fact," he added as they emerged back onto the first floor, "it's a registered landmark building, so even if we wanted to, we couldn't tear it down."

When they came to the front door, Melissa took one last glance back at the shadowy interior. A shudder passed through her, as though some indefinable evil that lurked within the building's dark stone walls were making its presence known. "I don't know," she said, shaking the feeling off, "I guess sometimes I just wonder if places like this should really be saved. It's as if so much unhappiness lived here that it seeped into the walls themselves. And I wonder if anything we do will ever really change that."

Bill McGuire glanced anxiously at the banker. "You're not changing your mind about the loan, are you?" he asked.

Melissa hesitated, then chuckled. "No," she assured him. "I'm not. I'm just musing, that's all. As a person, the whole place gives me the willies. But as a banker, I have to say it looks like a terrific investment."

A moment later they drove out of the Asylum grounds, totally unaware that only a few minutes before, Oliver Metcalf had stood on the porch, waiting for them—then fled.

The headache slowly eased, the nausea passed, and the black veil of terror that had fallen over Oliver lifted.

Yet he was still nearly blind, for only a faint glimmer of starlight broke the darkness that surrounded him.

He was running. But where? And from what?

His foot struck something. Tripping, he lunged uncontrollably forward, then sprawled facedown on the ground.

Instinctively throwing his right hand out to break his fall, it too struck something—something hard and rough—and a second later his other hand found something else. Gasping to catch his breath, fighting the urge to leap to his feet once again and flee whatever nameless thing might be pursuing him, he made himself stay on the ground, forced himself not to give in again to the panic that had overcome him on the Asylum steps, and concentrated on calming his fraying nerves.

There's nothing, he told himself. *Nothing chasing you. Nothing to be afraid of. Nothing at all!*

As his breathing and pulse slowly returned to normal, he sat up, reached out, and finally understood where he was.

The cemetery.

The little plot of land where for nearly half a century the unclaimed bodies of patients whose families had abandoned them to the confines of the Asylum's walls had been laid to rest once their tortured journeys through life had finally come to an end.

A potter's field, really, for it was as filled with the

homeless and the friendless as any other paupers' grave-yard might be.

Except that not only the long-forgotten patients of the Asylum had been buried here.

Finally getting to his feet, Oliver found himself thread-ing his way among the weathered granite grave markers toward the far corner, where, in a small area set off by a rusting wrought-iron fence, his father was buried. Paus-ing at the gate, he gazed down at the headstone that was barely visible beneath the night sky.

> Malcolm Metcalf
> Born February 25, 1914
> Died March 19, 1959

Why had his father killed himself?

And why had he chosen to die on that particular date?

Always—since he was a small boy—Oliver had as-sumed his father had chosen the date out of grief for his lost child.

But what if it had been something else?

Oliver didn't know; would probably never know.

Even now, nearly forty years later, he remembered practically nothing of any of it.

Whatever memories he had were buried as deeply in his subconscious as his father was buried in the dark, cold ground.

For a long time Oliver stood in the quiet of the night, staring down at the grave marker. Then snatches of the medical record he'd read only a little while ago began to drift through his mind.

Restraints . . . ice-cold baths . . . electroconvulsive therapy.

"What did you do, Father?" The words forming in his mind were barely audible on his lips. But then, as the import of the question grew, he repeated it aloud: "What did you do?"

Still the question swelled, taking on the force of a drumbeat, growing louder, louder in his mind, and once more he uttered it. This time, though, it wasn't a whisper. This time it was a howl of anguish, bellowed into the darkening night.

"WHAT DID YOU DO?"

Chapter 5

Germaine Wagner huddled in her bed, her blanket wrapped around her, struggling against the panic that had overwhelmed her in the front parlor. She had neither turned on the light when she came into the room nor changed into her nightgown before retreating to the bed, so terrified was she of what she might see in the bright light of the chandelier, or hidden in the shadows of her closet. For a time—a long time—she sat trembling in the darkness, her heart pounding so hard she could hear nothing else, the vein in her forehead pulsing so strongly she feared she might have a stroke.

But as the endless minutes ticked by, the adrenaline in her blood began to be reabsorbed and her pulse to calm. As she emerged from the shock of her terror, her wits slowly came back to her and she began consciously to try to relax, to ease the tension that had led her to draw her legs up against her chest and to wrap her arms tightly around her knees.

This is not me, she told herself. *I don't react like this. Not to anything.*

But a second later, as her memory released a vision of the flies and gnats that had swarmed around her, and the snakes that writhed on the floor of the parlor, another wave of panic towered over her. This time, though, Germaine retained her self-control.

It didn't happen, she silently insisted. Whatever it was, I only imagined it.

Germaine Wagner knew she was not the type to imagine things. She had always prided herself on her ability to see things clearly, and exactly as they were. Even when she'd been a child and her playmates had gazed up into the sky to envision elephants and tigers and other wondrous creatures soaring overhead, Germaine had seen nothing but stratus, cumulus, and cumulonimbus clouds drifting on the wind. The mind, she knew, was intended to be an analytical tool, and she believed in keeping it well honed, abstaining from ingesting any chemical that might interfere with its workings. She had never had a drink, never smoked a marijuana cigarette, and had certainly never experimented with any of the drugs that—

Drugs?

She turned the possibility over in her mind. Was it possible that Rebecca Morrison might have put something in the tea? Of course it was!

It was Rebecca's revenge, a spiteful reaction for having taken the handkerchief from her before she could ruin it!

As her fear gave way to anger, Germaine touched the pocket of her blouse to be certain the handkerchief was still there. It would have been just like Rebecca to snatch it from her pocket while she was still under the influence of whatever substance the ungrateful girl had put into the tea. Finding that the handkerchief was still there, Germaine slipped it out of the pocket of her blouse and into her bra.

Her anger, though, was unassuaged. Obviously it had been a mistake to take Rebecca into her home. To repay her kindness—not to mention her mother's!—with such a trick was unconscionable. Utterly unacceptable. Rebecca would simply have to find another place to live.

The decision made—and made unalterably, as were all her decisions—Germaine saw no point in putting off telling Rebecca that she would have to find another place to stay.

Tonight would be the girl's last under her roof.

Throwing back the blanket, Germaine started to rise, and then she heard a noise.

A faint scratching sound, as if something were trying to claw through the screen outside her window. Satisfied that she'd identified the sound, Germaine sat up and swung her feet off the bed.

The sound came again, only this time it wasn't outside her window.

It was in the room.

A tiny clicking and scraping noise, as if something— something small—had scurried across the bare hardwood that was exposed around the edges of the antique rag rug that covered most of the floor.

A mouse?

Germaine's feet jerked reflexively, then went firmly back down as she realized her terror had driven her into her bed without even taking off her shoes. As she stood, she heard the skittering sound again. This time, though, she ignored it, reaching for the electrified hurricane lamp that sat on her night table. She switched it on, and the warm glow of its light banished the darkness.

For just a moment Germaine relaxed. But then she heard the scampering again, and saw a flicker of motion out of the corner of her eye. She jerked her head toward the movement so quickly that she felt a spasm of pain in her neck, and reached up to rub at the spot.

Something wriggled under her fingers!

She turned again, frantically trying to brush away the thing on her neck, and this time caught a glimpse of herself in the mirror above her dresser.

A centipede, its dozens of tiny legs moving in smooth waves, was creeping up her neck. Gasping, Germaine brushed it off and tried to step on it, but it disappeared under the bed.

Dropping to her hands and knees, she lifted the bed's skirt and peered beneath the metal frame, reaching for her slipper, intent on smashing the repulsive little creature.

But her slipper was gone. In its place was a large rat, its red eyes glaring at her, hissing as it crouched, ready to leap. Her heart racing, a tiny shriek escaped Germaine's lips as she jerked her hand back. Then she saw another movement out of the corner of her eye, and lost her balance as she ducked away. As she sprawled out onto the rug, she felt something brush against her hair.

She rolled over, panic welling up uncontrollably, and tried to get to her feet. With a rush, something darted at her out of the corner of the room—a bat, she thought—and she ducked away again. Her foot catching on the rug, she plunged forward, her forehead smashing against the edge of her dresser.

A jagged spear of pain slashed through her head, and when she rubbed at the sore spot, she felt the warm stickiness of blood. A cry as much of fear as of pain erupted from her throat. Terrified, she tried to struggle to her feet.

Now the bat was back, fluttering around her head. She tried to swat it away but it swooped in close to her, then disappeared into the folds of the curtains that covered her window. Groping for something—anything—with which to protect herself from the bat, Germaine's hand closed on an alabaster pot of face powder. She hurled it at the spot where she was certain she'd seen the bat. It smashed against the window, shattering into a hundred pieces, sending a cloud of powder boiling up from the broken pot, releasing a swarm of gnats and flies, countless times the number that had risen from the chocolate box downstairs. Millions of them, a dense, dark, choking cloud that swirled toward her. A moan of terror erupted from Germaine's throat, and she backed away from the dark swarm, screaming, choking as they invaded her open mouth. Coughing, beating them back with flailing arms, she dropped to her hands and knees.

Hundreds of mice ran out from under the bed; Germaine jerked her hands away as they stampeded over her fingers. Her knuckles smashed against the metal bed frame, tearing the skin away. As her stinging fingers began to bleed, the rat darted out into the open. Grabbing the bed lamp, Germaine smashed it down at the rodent. The glass shattered against the floor, shards flying up into her face, lacerating her skin.

The air was thick with insects, alive with bats, their wings beating, sharp teeth bared. With a scream that emerged as no more than a gagging sound, Germaine struggled to her feet and stumbled to her bathroom, slammed the door behind her, then groped for the light switch.

Brilliant white light flooded the room. Germaine stared into the mirror over the sink. But what she saw bore no resemblance to her own image. A gargoyle's face stared back at her, blood oozing from its eyes, worms clinging to its cheeks. As it opened its toothless mouth, a serpent erupted from the dark hole, striking out at her with dripping fangs as the monster in the mirror reached out with clawed and scaled fingers.

With her own fists, Germaine smashed the mirror, sending broken glass cascading to the sink and floor. A glimmering scimitar slashed at her leg as it fell, then tumbled onward, glistening with blood, only to shatter on the tiles.

Every droplet of her blood seemed to come alive so that the floor was crawling with red ants. Germaine sank to her knees, sobbing, helplessly watching as the ants swarmed over her skin, feeling the fire of their millions upon millions of bites.

Crawling out of the bathroom, she lurched once more to her feet and staggered toward the door, finally escaping from her room onto the mezzanine. She peered over the balustrade, gazing down into the vast entry hall below. Where the huge Oriental carpet had been spread all her life, now Germaine saw nothing but a terrifying pit filled with writhing snakes.

Sinking to her knees, she vomited onto the floor. The contents of her stomach spewed from her mouth, instantly turning into wriggling maggots and pulsing slugs, spreading around her, then turning to creep back toward her.

Out!

She had to get out!

But there was no way out, no escape save the staircase that led down to the pit of vipers.

There was no choice. Everywhere she looked, she saw some new threat advancing on her. She edged backward, her throat burning with acid, her stomach heaving. At the top of the stairs she peered down.

The steps cascaded away from her, dropping endlessly, the bottom unreachably far away.

She hesitated, and something dropped from the ceiling into her hair.

Twisting her neck to look up, she saw the spiders.

They were everywhere, their webs hanging from the chandelier and the skylight, covering the walls and the moldings. The spiders, black and shiny, the red hour-glasses on their underbellies glimmering brightly, crept toward her.

She could hear their mandibles clicking, see the drops of poison that soon would be coursing through her veins.

Whimpering, nearly insane with fear, Germaine Wagner began scrabbling her way down the stairs toward the writhing mass of serpents that waited below.

Chapter 6

Though the graveyard that adjoined the Congregational church was surrounded by no less than four of Blackstone's old-fashioned streetlights, none of them cast enough illumination into the two-acre plot to penetrate the shadows in its center. Oliver paused as he came to the gate in the white picket fence, wondering if the headache that had been plaguing him all day would strike again.

Across the street someone was making his way through the square, but from where Oliver stood, the figure was no more than an indistinct dark silhouette that soon disappeared entirely. Suddenly feeling oddly exposed even in the dim glow cast by the converted gas lamps, Oliver stepped through the gate, closed it behind him, and made his way along the paths that twisted between the gravestones until he came to the weathered marble mausoleum that Charles Connally had built in 1927, when he and every one of his five sisters had made up their minds that they would not be buried in the edifice their father had already constructed for himself, his wife, and their six offspring.

An edifice in which old Jonas Connally—Harvey Connally's grandfather and Oliver's great-grandfather—had deliberately provided no space for the men his daughters had married, let alone Charles's wife or any of their progeny.

To this day, the bodies of Jonas and Charity Connally lay in lonely splendor in an immense white limestone building at the exact center of the cemetery, their mausoleum empty save for the two of them.

Their son and daughters—along with their own husbands, Charles's wife Eleanor, and at least a few of every generation of their further descendants—were housed in six separate edifices, each of them built so that it faced away from the structure that Jonas Connally had erected, an eternal reminder that just as they had in life finally turned their backs on the patriarch of the Connally clan, so also had they turned away from him in death.

Oliver had always thought there was something almost inexpressibly sad in the manner in which the arrangement of the mausoleums bore eternal testament to the long-forgotten grudge that had existed between Jonas Connally, his son, Charles, and his five daughters, but of all the structures, he found the one built by Charles, Oliver's own grandfather and the man who had erected the great mansion on North Hill, to be the saddest.

Though Charles Connally died long before Oliver had been born, his uncle Harvey had often told him of the elder Connally's unflagging enthusiasm and optimism, which had extended even to the mausoleum he'd constructed with enough space for himself and his wife Eleanor, his children and their spouses, and a dozen grandchildren as well. But even after all these years, only four of the mausoleum's crypts were occupied—and, Oliver thought grimly, only two more ever would be.

The pale marble structure glowed in the dim light, almost as if it were lit from within rather than by the four distant streetlights. As he approached it, Oliver gazed at the motto that had been etched deeply in the marble that formed the three steps leading to the crypts:

ALL ARE WELCOMED — NONE COMMANDED

Still another rebuke to his great-grandfather. As he did every time he read the words, Oliver wondered if he would ever know what the quarrel between Jonas and his children had truly been about.

That quarrel, though, had nothing to do with the reason he was here tonight. Mounting the steps, he stood facing the two crypts that were beneath and to the left of those occupied by his grandparents. Each of them bore a small plaque:

Olivia Connally Metcalf Born March 19, 1923 Died April 24, 1952	Mallory Connally Metcalf Born April 24, 1952 Died March 19, 1956

His mother and his sister, lying side by side.

He knew how his mother had died, of course. Giving birth to himself and Mallory proved to be too much for her, and in the end she lost her life so that both of her children might live.

A little girl, named for her husband.

A little boy, named for her.

The death of his sister, though, was as shrouded in mystery now as it had been on the day it occurred.

Pictures of both of them had been mounted into the stone, protected by thick glass, but long since faded to near invisibility. Yet Oliver knew every feature.

He reached out, laying his hand on his mother's image, and, as always happened, felt his eyes moisten with tears. "Why?" he whispered. "Why did you have to leave us?" He fell silent, as if waiting for an answer to his oft-asked question; the silence of the graveyard wrapped around him like an icy sheet, making him shiver in the darkness.

His hand moved to the image of his sister, whose death had occurred on what would have been their mother's thirty-third birthday.

This time a vision from the past came to his mind,

welling up from his memory as vividly as if he'd seen it all only yesterday.

He and Mallory were both very small—no more than three or so—and he was holding on to her hand as they ran across the lawn toward the forest. There was a spring in the woods, and the two of them used to love to go hide in the shrubbery that bordered the clear, racing stream and watch raccoons washing their food in the rushing water. Sometimes deer drank from its crystal surface.

If they were feeling particularly brave, he and Mallory would sometimes take off their shoes and socks and wade in the cold water welling out of the ground, even though their father had warned them that if they slipped and fell in, they could easily drown.

But they hadn't ever slipped; hadn't ever—

The stab of pain slashed through Oliver's head so suddenly that he staggered back from the crypt, and the vision of his sister vanished in the blackness that instantly closed around him.

A point of light appears in the blackness.

The boy stares at it. As he focuses his mind on it, the point slowly begins to expand.

Now it is as if he is looking into a tunnel.

At the end of the tunnel he sees a coffin.

The boy emerges from the tunnel. He is in a church, staring at a coffin.

A small coffin.

Small enough that even he would barely fit in it.

Hands lift him up, holding him high, so that he can look down into the coffin.

He sees a face.

His sister's face.

As he stares at it, his eyes wide, blood oozes from his sister's neck.

Shuddering as the headache slowly released him from its grip, Oliver pressed his hand against the glass covering his sister's image.

"Oh, God, why can't I remember? What's happening to me?" he cried, his voice breaking.

His eyes streaming with tears, his breath catching in his throat, Oliver turned away from the mausoleum and started the long walk back home.

Germaine had no idea how long it had taken her to descend the apparently endless staircase. Time itself lost its meaning as she flailed against the terrors that surrounded her. Cowering at the foot of the stairs, she gazed into the pit, mesmerized. What had been an enormous and lush Oriental carpet bearing an intricate pattern of flowers, vines, leaves and birds was now a pulsating, writhing, living mass that throbbed with a hypnotic rhythm and threatened to draw her irretrievably into its deadly grasp. Vines grew before her very eyes, their tendrils reaching out to twist around her ankles. Snakes slithered among the vines, their undulating bodies nearly indistinguishable from the sinews of the plants themselves. A whimper escaped Germaine's lips as she tried to turn away from the hideous vision, but the jungle before her held her in its thrall.

A glistening drop of saliva oozed from the corner of her mouth, but Germaine was as oblivious to it as she now was to the blood that dripped from the gashes on her legs.

The jungle dropped away, consumed by the black bottomless pit that opened before her. A wave of vertigo struck Germaine as she stared into the abyss, and she flung one arm out to try to steady herself, succeeding only in smashing her hand against the hard wood of the newel-post at the base of the stairs. The sudden bone-jarring pain in her hand cost her what little was left of her equilibrium. Her balance deserted her.

Screaming, she plunged into the blackness far below. As she fell she could see the writhing snakes, their mouths gaping, fangs dripping with venom, straining upward as if to strike her even before she crashed to the ground.

Then they were all over her, twisting around her, binding her arms and legs. She couldn't breathe; her skin was crawling. Twisting. Turning. Screaming. Vipers churning over her. She tried to move her arms, her legs. Trapped. Immobile. Paralyzed. Screaming—screams of pain and terror. Then only utter despair.

Clara Wagner finally picked up the remote control and muted the volume on her television set. As the sound of the late news died away, the wailing from beyond her door became clearer, and her brow furrowed in irritation. What on earth was going on out there?

Was someone crying, or shouting?

It must be Germaine and Rebecca.

What on earth were they doing?

But of course she knew! Rebecca had undoubtedly done something stupid again, and Germaine would have corrected her. Now the silly child was crying. Well, it would have to stop.

Now.

Turning her chair toward the door, she rolled across the room, then struggled to open the heavy mahogany panel, one hand clutching the doorknob while she used the other to manipulate the chair's controls. As the door slowly swung open, the sounds grew louder. "For heaven's sake,"

Clara began as she rolled the chair out onto the broad mezzanine that encircled the huge entry hall below. "What on earth—"

The words died on her lips. Below her, she saw Germaine writhing on the carpet that was spread out over the broad expanse between the front door and the base of the stairs.

What in heaven's name was she doing? Had she fallen down the stairs?

"Germaine? *Germaine!*"

The screech echoing through the jungle galvanized Germaine. She lunged to her feet as she heard the as-yet-unseen beast crash toward her. Though the snakes still clung to her, and her vision was a red blur, with a preternatural strength born of sheer terror she jerked her limbs loose from the clutching vines and writhing vipers.

Hide.

She had to find someplace to hide.

Frantically turning first one way and then another, Germaine searched for someplace—anyplace—that would shelter her from the beast that was coming ever closer. Then, at last, she saw something.

A tree—a hollow tree.

Not much, but at least something.

The vines still dragging at her, the snakes still twisting around her, she struggled toward the shelter, finally dropping to all fours to slog her way across the mire the floor had become.

Then, as the beast roared again, she whimpered and redoubled her efforts.

*   *   *

"Germaine!"

Clara Wagner glared furiously down at her daughter. What on earth was she doing? Obviously she wasn't badly hurt, since she'd gotten up, taken a few steps, then dropped back down as if she were simply too dizzy to stand.

Dizzy!

Of course!

Germaine was drunk! That had to be it! After the scene she'd caused in the parlor, she'd gone back to her room and begun drinking.

It didn't surprise Clara—didn't surprise her at all. She'd always suspected Germaine was a secret drinker. Typical of the kind of person Germaine had turned out to be, despite how hard she had worked to raise her properly, and the sacrifices she'd made to make certain that Germaine had all the advantages. But the girl had always been a disappointment.

Maybe if she'd been pretty enough to snare a husband—

Too late now! Germaine would never be anything but an old-maid librarian.

But she would not be a drunk!

"I'm coming down there, Germaine!" Clara called over the edge of the mezzanine. "I'm coming down, and if I find out you've been drinking . . ."

She left the sentence hanging unfinished as she maneuvered the wheelchair toward the elevator. Angrily, she jerked at the accordion door of the brass cage. Finally pulling it open, she wheeled herself inside, then jabbed at the button that would send the cage down to the first floor.

The renewed roaring of the beast spurring her on, Germaine burst free of the vines and scrabbled across to the shelter of the hollow tree, no more than a rotting stump, its bark filled with holes. Drawing her knees to her breast and wrapping her arms around them, she closed her eyes and rocked back and forth. Her breath was coming in short gasps; every part of her body hurt now. Her skin felt as if millions of insects were crawling over it, and blood was smeared everywhere.

Sobbing and whimpering, she tried to shrink herself into an even smaller ball and clamp both her eyes and her ears shut against the terrors that surrounded her. Then a new sound penetrated the fog that was gathering in her mind.

A terrible clanking and groaning. The beast! Moving toward her. Against her will, she opened her eyes and looked up.

An enormous boulder—so huge it filled the entire hollowed trunk of the tree—was dropping toward her.

Germaine screamed in terror.

As her daughter's scream pierced the armor of anger in which Clara Wagner had wrapped herself, she realized with horror exactly where Germaine had chosen to hide from her mother's wrath. She reached out for the elevator's control, but the wheelchair had lodged itself against the back wall, one wheel jammed firmly into a crevice in the metal latticework, and her fingers hovered just short of the button that would stop the cage's descent. She fumbled wildly for the panel on the chair's right arm, but Clara's now-trembling fingers missed their target, and her heart began to beat erratically as she realized what was about to happen.

Then her fingers found the wheelchair's controls and pushed hard.

The motor hummed; the chair shuddered but did not

budge. The back wheel remained tightly jammed between the ornate ironwork struts of the cage.

Clara struggled harder, pushing at the cage itself in an effort to free the chair, but she had long ago let her muscles go far too flaccid to obey her commands now.

She leaned forward, stretching toward the elevator button, her heart racing wildly.

A stab of pain slashed through her head and her whole body stiffened. Then, as Germaine uttered yet another howl of pure terror, a great fist of pain smote Clara's head and she slumped in her chair.

Germaine's terrified howl rose into a scream of pure agony.

The cry built, rising through the great entry hall, expanding to fill the house. The air trembled with it, and then, so suddenly that even the silence that followed seemed to echo, it ended.

So also did the clanking of the elevator, and the grinding of the machine that ran it.

For a moment that seemed to stretch into eternity, silence reigned.

Then, as the pain that had crashed down on her slowly lifted, Clara Wagner moaned.

She tried to cry out—tried to call for help—but no words emerged from her lips.

Instead there was only an unintelligible stream of meaningless sound.

She tried to move.

As the worst terror she had ever felt closed around her, Clara Wagner realized that she was no longer in her wheelchair by choice.

Chapter 7

Rebecca was running, and even though she couldn't see her pursuer, she knew exactly what it was.

The dark figure, the same one she'd seen the night of the Hartwicks' party, moving silently down their driveway, then disappearing into the whirling snow so completely that it was almost as if he'd never been there at all.

But he was here tonight, chasing her. There was no way to escape him.

She was in the street, and there were houses on both sides, all of them brightly lit, all of them filled with people. But when Rebecca tried to scream, tried to call out for help, her throat constricted, and no sound emerged.

Her legs and feet seemed to work no better than her voice. Though she was running as hard as she could, she was barely moving at all, for her feet felt as if they were mired in mud, and every muscle in her legs ached from exhaustion. And every second the dark figure was looming closer to her.

Suddenly, the houses around her disappeared, leaving her in utter darkness. Terror clutching at her throat, she sensed the threatening figure lurch ever closer, and she redoubled her efforts, plunging through the darkness, unheeding of where she might be running to, so long as she was escaping her pursuer.

Now she felt hands reaching out, grasping at her, and

she tried to pull away, but the hands closed on her, and then she fell, a muffled scream escaping her lips, and—

Rebecca listened to the rapid beating of her heart, a thudding in the silence of the house.

She had no idea what time it was, no idea how long she'd slept. After taking the tea things back to the kitchen and retreating to her room, she'd stretched out on her bed, intending only to close her eyes for a minute or two—to try to relax—but when she'd jerked awake from the nightmare a few minutes ago, her mind was as foggy as if she'd been sleeping for hours. She wasn't even certain whether the muffled cry that ended her sleep had come from somewhere downstairs or only been the end of the terrible dream in which—

But the dream had vanished from her mind, every detail of it erased so completely that had she not still been in the last, weakening clutches of its terror, she might have wondered if she'd had the dream at all. Yet she was sure it was the nightmare that had awakened her, and as the mist in her mind slowly cleared away, other sounds filtered in. A few minutes ago she'd heard a crash coming from the second floor.

She'd almost gone downstairs to investigate. Then she remembered the beautiful handkerchief that Oliver had given her, and that Germaine had promptly snatched away to give to her mother. *It doesn't matter,* she told herself. *Germaine has been very kind to you, and if she wanted the handkerchief for Miss Clara, you shouldn't begrudge it.* But when Miss Clara hadn't wanted it after all, why had Germaine insisted on keeping it for herself?

Even so, she reminded herself, *if something is wrong downstairs, you should go see if you can help.*

Still she hesitated, the strange scene she'd witnessed in the parlor fresh in her memory. What had come over

Germaine? From the moment she'd opened the box of chocolates, it had been as if . . .

Even in the privacy of her own mind, Rebecca hesitated to use the word that had popped into her head. Yet there was no other way to describe it.

It was as if Germaine suddenly had gone crazy.

Although it had been no more than a minute or two before Germaine fled the room, the scene had terrified Rebecca. When she'd taken the tea tray back to the kitchen, her hands were trembling so badly that she was afraid she might drop it. And she still had no idea at all what had happened to Germaine.

She recalled, then, hearing glass breaking, followed by a sound that was part scream and part moan. Had she not been so badly frightened by the terrible scene in the parlor, Rebecca knew she would have hurried to see what had happened.

But what if Germaine really had gone crazy? What if she would have attacked her?

The house had fallen silent for a few minutes, but then the noise started up again. She heard Miss Clara shouting, and decided that Germaine was no longer in her room and that she and her mother must be having a fight. Better not to interfere, she'd thought.

For the first time since she'd awakened, Rebecca felt the tension in her body ease a little. When she heard the grinding of the gears that operated the elevator, Rebecca concluded that the argument must be over.

A sudden scream—a scream so terrifying it made Rebecca's blood run cold—erupted through the house. At almost exactly the same instant, the elevator's machinery fell silent.

Finally, the terrible quiet.

It held Rebecca in a strange thrall. She stood motionless at her bedside, one hand on the iron footboard, straining to hear anything that might reveal whatever terrible tragedy had brought forth that final, awful, ear-splitting scream.

The silence seemed to turn into a living thing, taking on a terrifying, suffocating quality, and slowly it came to Rebecca that only she could end it. Unconsciously holding her breath, she finally gathered her courage to leave her room and walk to the top of the steep and narrow flight of stairs leading down to the second floor.

Her steps echoing hollowly, she descended the bare wood stairs and gazed down into the hall below. Though she saw nothing, she sensed that it was not empty.

It was as she started toward the head of the great sweeping staircase at the far end of the mezzanine that the silence was finally broken.

A sound—nothing more than a gurgling whimper—drifted up from below.

As she came to the elevator shaft, Rebecca paused and peered down. A glistening pool of blood was spreading across the floor in front of the elevator door.

Her heart pounding now, Rebecca ran to the head of the stairs. For one terrible moment she hesitated, instinctively knowing that whatever awaited her below was going to be far worse than anything she might be able to imagine, and wanting desperately to turn away from it, to go back to her room, to hide herself from whatever horror had transpired below.

But she knew she couldn't. Whatever it was had to be faced.

Gathering her strength, Rebecca walked down the stairs and gazed upon the elevator.

Clara Wagner was slumped in her wheelchair inside the cage. Her eyes were open and seemed to be staring at Rebecca, but her jaw hung slack, and spittle dripped from the corner of her mouth.

Rebecca was certain she was dead.

The pool of blood was still spreading out from beneath

the elevator, and for one brief instant Rebecca failed to understand exactly what had happened.

Then she saw it.

From beneath the narrow space between the bottom of the elevator and the floor itself, an arm protruded.

Clutched in the fingers of the hand, Rebecca saw the handkerchief.

The handkerchief that Oliver had given her.

Her mind utterly numbed by the terrible vision spread before her, Rebecca moved across the broad sweep of the Oriental carpet, bent down and reached for the handkerchief.

Germaine Wagner's fingers, even in death, seemed to tighten on the scrap of linen for a moment, but then relaxed.

Suddenly, a stream of strangled, unintelligible sounds gurgled out of Clara Wagner's throat.

Jumping as if she'd received a jolt of electricity, Rebecca gasped, then whirled to face the old woman in the wheelchair.

Clara Wagner's eyes were glowing malevolently now, and the fingers of her right hand were twitching spasmodically, as if she were still trying to make her wheelchair respond to her bidding.

Terrified by the specter of the old woman who seemed to have come back from the dead before her very eyes, Rebecca backed away a step or two, then fled out into the night.

Help!

She had to find help!

She ran down the sidewalk into the street, then hesitated, wondering where to go.

Oliver!

If she could just get to Oliver, he would be able to help her!

Racing to the corner, she started up Amherst Street.

And the memory of the dream—the memory that had

vanished so completely when she'd awakened only a little while ago—came flooding back.

A terrible, unreasoning panic rose in Rebecca, and suddenly she was caught up in the nightmare once more. The darkness of the night closed around her; even the houses on either side of the street seemed to shrink away, retreating beyond her reach.

Once more her feet seemed to be mired in sludge, and every muscle in her legs was aching.

Now she could feel a presence—a terrifying, evil presence—close behind her.

She opened her mouth to cry out, to scream for someone to help her, but just as in the dream, her throat was constricted and no sound emerged.

Her heart pounding, her lungs failing her, she forced her legs to move, lunging up the hill into the darkness.

An arm reached out of the darkness, sliding around her neck, and then, as she finally found her voice, a hand clamped over her mouth.

A hand made slick by a latex glove.

Chapter 8

*T*he dark figure prowled the cold stone building like a panther patrolling his domain, every nerve on edge, every muscle tense.

He could sense the trespassers everywhere; it was as if their very scent was in the air. Every room they had entered seemed somehow violated, as if that which was rightfully his had been taken away.

Yet nothing was gone.

Everything was exactly as it had been before, save for the dust that was disturbed as they tramped from one room to another.

Opening doors they had no right to open.

Touching things that were never meant for any fingers but his own.

Peering into every closet and drawer, trying to ferret out his secrets.

What right had they to invade his realm?

He tracked them as easily as a carnivore stalking its prey, knowing where they'd been with as much certainty as if they were still there, and he were slinking after them, watching them with a wary eye.

The third floor was where they'd spent the least of their time, barely stopping at some of the rooms, entering only a few. But why not? There was nothing much here—never had been.

What little it contained were castoffs, things of little interest and even smaller value.

They'd explored the rooms on the second floor more thoroughly, entering every one, running their fingers over every object—*his* objects.

He sensed at once what they were doing, of course.

Placing values on every object they found, trying to determine what each one might be worth. But what did it matter what the building's contents were worth?

The things within the Asylum were not theirs to sell.

All of it—every bit of it!—was his.

It wasn't so bad on the ground floor. The rooms on that floor, shielded from the world outside by the two great oaken doors, had always been filled with strangers, and the three who had been there that day made little difference. Indeed, as he moved quickly through the rooms, it was almost as if their presence had made no difference at all.

It was in the lowest rooms of all, the chambers that had been hidden away in the basement by purposeful design, that he most sharply felt the ravages of the invasion that had taken place that day.

Their voices seemed still to echo within the tiled walls of those wondrous chambers in which the work had been performed. As he moved from one to another, remembering perfectly the specific use for which each had been designed, the rage simmering within him began to boil, for he knew deep within his soul that the interlopers had not looked upon these rooms with the respect they deserved.

They had been repulsed by what they found here. Even now their condemnation hung like a poisonous vapor in the air. As he completed his inspection, his indignation swelled, for he knew that despite what they had felt, these petty, conniving fools had no real idea at all of what transpired in these rooms, to what uses these sacred spaces had actually been put.

How, he wondered, would they feel if they truly understood?

Well, soon they would, for he was going to show them.

With satisfaction, he tested the concealed entrance to the most important room of all, and found it undisturbed.

This room, still, was known to no one but himself.

This room, which contained his most cherished treasures.

From one of the shelves he took a large mahogany box, and set it on the table. Opening the box, he lifted an ancient stereoscope from the larger of the box's two compartments, and a stack of curled and yellowed cards from the smaller. Gently placing one of the cards in the rack at one end of the stereoscope, he held the instrument to his eyes and peered through the lenses.

There was just enough light filtering through the window from the waning moon to illuminate the image.

Before him was an old-fashioned room, filled with overstuffed sofas and chairs, and ornate tables covered with bric-a-brac. The illusion of three dimensions was so perfect that he almost felt as if he might be able to reach into the room itself, pick up one of the objects, and handle it.

But of course he couldn't.

After all, the stereoscope was only an amusement, and the images it offered no more than illusions of reality.

Still, it was a toy that would make a perfect gift. . . .

To be continued . . .

The serial thriller continues next month . . .

JOHN SAUL'S
THE BLACKSTONE CHRONICLES
Part Five
Day of Reckoning: The Stereoscope

Blackstone is being stalked by a menacing, unknown force. People in this once-peaceful town are suffering unspeakable fates—and one beloved citizen has tragically disappeared. What terrible curse is being played out in this small corner of New England? Who will become the next link in this ferocious chain of evil: The local contractor Bill McGuire . . . Sheriff Steve Driver . . . prominent attorney Ed Becker . . . his loving wife, Bonnie, or their daughter, Amy? Or will Oliver Metcalf be next?

This time, the mysterious object is a stereo-scope, an antique instrument that allows you to see images in three dimensions. And brings terror into a new, unspeakable shape . . .

To be continued . . .

THE PRESENCE
by John Saul

When *New York Times* bestselling author John Saul creates a story, you can rest assured you're in the hands of a proven master of psychological and supernatural suspense. But his latest novel of terror out-scares anything he has ever written before. For once you've felt the sheer evil, the unstoppable sensation of *The Presence*, you may never see the light of day again. . . .

Beware of
The Presence

Coming in July 1997
A Fawcett Columbine Hardcover Book

JOIN THE CLUB!